BOOKS BY CLAIRE COOK

Must Love Dogs (#1)
Must Love Dogs: New Leash on Life (#2)
Must Love Dogs: Fetch You Later (#3)

Never Too Late: Your Roadmap to Reinvention

Life's a Beach
The Wildwater Walking Club
Summer Blowout
Multiple Choice
Time Flies
Wallflower in Bloom
Best Staged Plans
Seven Year Switch
Ready to Fall

and coming soon . . .
lots more Must Love Dogs!

PRAISE FOR MUST LOVE DOGS

"This utterly charming novel by Cook is a fun read,
perfect for whiling away an afternoon on the beach."
—*Library Journal*

"Funny and pitch perfect."—*Chicago Tribune*

"Wildly witty"—*USA Today*

"Cook dishes up plenty of charm."
—*San Francisco Chronicle*

"A hoot"—*The Boston Globe*

"[A] laugh-out-loud novel . . . a light and lively read for
anyone who has ever tried to re-enter the dating scene
or tried to 'fix up' somebody else."—*Boston Herald*

"Reading *Must Love Dogs* is like having lunch with
your best friend—fun, breezy, and full of laughs."
—*Lorna Landvik*

"A hilariously original tale about dating and its place in
a modern woman's life."—*BookPage*

"Funny and quirky and honest."—*Jane Heller*

"Claire Cook's novel *Must Love Dogs* was such a huge success that it was made into a hit movie starring Diane Lane and John Cusack. Now Cook is back with *Must Love Dogs: New Leash on Life*, which proves just as delightful."
—*Nancy Lepri, New York Journal of Books*

(5 stars!) "If you haven't read a Claire Cook book yet, start with this one. You don't need to have read the first book, but why not grab that one, too, and read it? Her books are like potato chips – you can't have just one!"—*Pamela Kramer, National Book Reviewer, Examiner.com*

"If *Must Love Dogs* is any indication of her talents, readers will hope that Claire Cook will be telling breezy stories from the South Shore of Massachusetts for seasons to come."
—*The Washington Post*

"A wry look at contemporary courtship rituals, as well as a warm portrayal of a large Irish-American family."—*St. Louis Post-Dispatch*

Must Love Dogs

Fetch You Later (#3)

Claire Cook

Marshbury Beach Books

Marshbury Beach Books
Book Layout: The Book Designer
Cover Photo: Kris Holland
Author Photo: Kaden Jacobucci

Must Love Dogs: Fetch You Later/ Claire Cook
ISBN 978-1-942671-10-7

For My Readers

One

"Here we go again," Carol said from the backseat.

My sisters Carol and Christine and I were on our way to our family home to meet our father's latest girlfriend. Our father had summoned us. I was driving. Christine was still mad at us for leaving her out of our last adventure, so Carol was uncharacteristically sitting in the backseat and letting Christine ride shotgun.

Because everybody with any sense at all was at the beach, we had the Marshbury back roads practically to ourselves. The light up ahead of us turned yellow. I accelerated, changed my mind, hit the brake. Tried not to think that there might be a metaphor in there somewhere about the way I lived my life.

I rolled down my window, hoping for a sea breeze. Soggy August air pushed past the wall of air-conditioning, on a mission to frizz my hair. I hit the button again and listened to the window chug its way back up.

While we waited for the light to change, I checked up on my hair. The signs of frizz were undeniable and almost enough to make me yearn for the crisp fall air. Except for the fact that I was a teacher.

"I can't believe summer is practically over," Carol said. "I am counting the *milliseconds* till the kids are back in school."

"Don't," I said. "Please don't."

"Dad sounded pretty excited about this Sally when I talked to him," Christine said.

"Now there's something new," Carol said. "Dad excited about a woman."

I clicked the blinker of my trusty old Honda Civic, took a right past a canopy of sugar maples. I pretended not to notice that a few random leaves were already changing color.

"A rose by any other name and all that," I said, "but you have to admit Sally sounds like a step up from *Sugar Butt*."

Christine sighed. "I can't believe I still feel left out that I missed meeting someone named Sugar Butt."

Carol reached forward to give her a pat on the shoulder. "You'll get over it, Chris. And just so you're completely looped in, Ms. Butt was definitely a step up from Dolly."

"Dolly," we groaned.

"Marlene was the classiest," I said. "And her casseroles were amazing, even if she did have them delivered by her caterer."

"It's the thought that counts," Christine said.

"Actually," I said, "it's the casserole that counts." I relied on my father's date-baked casseroles to supplement my own pathetic cooking skills.

"Well," Carol said, "at least he's finally using the laptop we bought him instead of that clickety-clackety old typewriter. One can only hope that online dating will improve the demographics."

"As well as the casseroles," I said.

"I can't believe Michael didn't come with us today," Christine said. "I mean, Billy Jr. and Johnny bail on us all the time, but Michael's—"

"Practically a sister," Carol said.

"I think we have to cut him some slack," I said. "Now that Phoebe and the girls are finally back home, he doesn't want to blow it."

We offered up a moment of silence for our brother Michael's bumpy marriage. My praying skills weren't much better than my cooking skills, but for what it was worth I threw in a quick Hail Mary anyway.

When we pulled into the driveway of the 1890 Victorian all five of my sisters and brothers and I had grown up in, my entire childhood flashed before my eyes the way it always did. Every firefly caught in a jar. Every mad dash through the sprinkler. Every slam of the warped wooden screen door. Every date that braved his way across the moat-like wraparound porch to knock on the massive oak front door—not that there were all that many of them.

"Come on," Carol said, "let's get this over with. Dennis promised the kids we'd hit the beach after dinner so they could fly their kites."

"Ooh, that's a good idea," Christine said. "Kite-flying always tires them out. Maybe we'll meet you there."

We crunched across the crushed mussel shell drive-way, clumped our way up the steps and across the wraparound porch. Carol gave a quick knock, turned the old brass doorknob. "How many times do we have to tell him to lock the door . . ."

"He'd probably just give everyone he met a key," I said.

"Da-ad," Christine yelled. "Your favorite daughters are here."

A pile of boxes greeted us in the entryway.

"Jeez Louise," I whispered. "His girlfriends sure don't travel light, do they?"

Christine was already squatting down to read one of the boxes. "A case of Depends? Whoa, they're certainly not getting any younger."

Carol put on her reading glasses and leaned over another box. "A 48-piece knife collection? You don't think he's taken up knife throwing, do you?"

"Right," Christine said. She dropped her voice to a whisper. "The new girlfriend balances an apple on her head, and then Dad chooses a knife and lets it rip."

"Come on, you guys," I said. "Don't be rude." I lifted the flap of another box, which had already been opened so therefore didn't register on the rude-ometer.

I pulled out a can. "Dog food? He doesn't even have a dog."

Our father stepped into view, raking his mane of disheveled white hair with one hand.

We took turns giving him a hug while we waited for his new girlfriend to materialize.

"Where is she?" I finally asked.

"'She walks in beauty,'" our father said, "'like the night/Of cloudless climes and starry skies/And all that's best of dark and bright/Meet in her aspect and in her eyes.'" He turned and drifted off in the direction of the kitchen, as if he were exiting stage left.

My sisters and I looked at one another. "Browning?" Christine said.

"I don't think so," Carol said. "It might be Yeats."

I shook my head. "It's totally Tennyson." I lowered my voice. "Why do you think his new girlfriend didn't come out to greet us?"

"She's probably powdering her nose so she can impress us," Christine said.

Carol shrugged. "Maybe you should take a quick peek around, Sarah. Just so we know what we're dealing with this time around."

"Me?" I said. "Why should I be the one who has to peek? I drove."

Carol made a beeline for the kitchen. Christine was right behind her.

Since my sisters had left me no choice but to play Nancy Drew, I took the scenic route, running my hand along the worn mahogany banister as I passed the center staircase. I glanced up at the gallery of family photos above the stairs, trying to ignore the gap, like a missing tooth, where my old wedding photo used to hang.

I reached for the old cut glass doorknob that led to the back room we once used as a guestroom-slash-den-slash-playroom. Sleuthing away, I opened the door a crack. A pile of clothing claimed the bed. It looked like at least some of it still had the tags on. For the first time it occurred to me that maybe the women my father brought home never made it upstairs to the master bedroom.

I hadn't set foot in our parents' bedroom since about a month after our mother's funeral. We'd finally made ourselves split up the pieces of clothing we wanted to keep to remind us of her. We spent the rest of the day crying and packing up everything else to donate to a women's shelter. A part of me hoped our father had turned their bedroom into a shrine to our mother: votive candles surrounding framed photos on every available surface. Another part of me wondered if he'd simply moved to another bedroom, the way I'd relocated from my own master bedroom when my former husband Kevin moved out.

I had absolutely no urge to climb the stairs to see if my parents' bedroom showed signs of occupancy, or even cohabitation. Unlike Nancy Drew, sometimes I really didn't want a clue.

When I got to the kitchen, my father and Carol were sitting at the scarred pine trestle table. A towering stack of boxes on the other side of the kitchen blocked the single glass door to the patio. The counters were littered with smaller boxes and padded envelopes, some opened, some not. Our father's laptop sat on the middle of the table, its charging cord stretched like a mini-clothesline to the nearest plug.

Christine was pulling bottles of iced tea from one of the boxes. I yanked open another box. Beet juice. I held out my hand for an iced tea.

"You want to tell us what's going on, Dad?" Carol said. "I mean, you practically order us to come over and meet your new girlfriend, and then she doesn't even wait around for us?"

"She's not one to sit still for long, our Sally." Our father put one hand over his heart and sighed. "But I'm smitten with that kitten."

Two

"So now what?" I said.

By way of answer, our father woke up his laptop. "Hot diggity dog, will you look at that. An Alaska cruise for two *and* a year's supply of those new-fangled light bulbs. And that's just since the last time I checked the internut."

I started to correct my father, then let it go, the way I sometimes did when one of the kids in my class said *cimmamum* or *jawamas*. A little bit of cute never hurt anything.

Christine leaned over so she could see the screen. "You're entering sweepstakes now? When did that start?"

Our father took a break from his two-fingered typing. "When you get to be my age, Carol—"

"Christine," she said.

"There are lots of hours in the day that need filling." He stretched, leaned back in his chair, laced his fingers behind his head. "And truth be told, it's been the bees knees to feel like a winner again." He raised his iced tea in our direction. "I reeled in five entire cases of these babies. Sun-brewed, no less."

"To the spoils of victory," I said. We all clanked bottles.

"You're always a winner to us, Dad," Carol said. "And if this *Sally* doesn't agree, we'll take her out."

I took a sip of warm iced tea. I had to admit it wasn't as good as the homemade stuff, and the aftertaste had a serious chemical tinge, but given that my father had gone to the trouble of winning it, I'd probably take my fair share home with me. If I got sick of it, I could always donate the rest to the teachers' room at school.

I pushed away the thought of yet another school year.

"Some of the other sweepers draw the line between sweepstakes and contests," our dad was saying. "But I'm not the kind of fellow who likes to discriminate, so personally I'm not opposed to writing a jingle or two on slow days."

Carol leaned over and pulled out a tube of bacon-flavored toothpaste from a carton on the floor. "You *tried* to win this?"

"And not to be rude," I said, "but what kind of sweepstakes has *beet juice* for a prize?"

"It all started . . ." Our dad shifted in his seat to get comfortable as he went into full story mode. " . . . when you kiddos made me retire my Smith Corona and take up with this laptopper here." He paused to give said laptopper a pat on the top of its shiny silver case.

"I thought you only used your laptop for online dating," Christine said.

He nodded. "And a lovely upgrade it was, thank you very much. But every time I'd set my sights on a fine young filly, something else entirely would pop up."

"Ick," I said.

"He means pop up ads," Carol said. "Jeesh, get your mind out of the gutter, Sarah."

Christine reached over and patted his hand. "Just ignore them. The pop up ads and my sisters."

He patted Christine's hand back. "At first I fiddled around until I found that sneaky little X way up in the corner that makes them go away, but one day I thought *what the hey*, and I filled out a doohickey or two, and then another—"

"Dad," I said. "Be careful. There are lots of scams out there—"

"Make sure you don't give out your personal info," Christine said. "Especially your social security number."

"Or anything else that's attached to our inheritance," Carol said.

He brushed our worries away with one hand. "Before I knew it, the postman was ringing my doorbell practically every day. Nothing better than the sweet sound of a doorbell ringing, is there now."

My sisters and I exchanged guilty looks. All six siblings stopped by to see our father as often as we could, together as well as individually, but sometimes life just got in the way.

Our dad took a slug of iced tea. "Meanwhile, back at the ranch, in what seemed a mere blink of an eye, I'd accumulated more doodads than any man needs. And then Angie, she's the mailman, thought perhaps if I began donating some of the spoils, it might do some good out in the world. And possibly reel in a bucket of luck for some bigger wins." He looked over his shoulder and lowered his voice. "I've got my heart set on that HGTV dream house."

"More tea?" he said. "We've got a sampler pack of the bag variety, too, and a case of some kind of agave nectar foolishness. Back in the day, tea was just tea. We kept things simple."

Carol turned her head casually so she could see the kitchen clock. Siobhan, her seventeen-year-old daughter, was babysitting for her three much younger siblings. I could practically watch the wheels in Carol's head turning as she calculated how much longer she could safely leave them before Siobhan decided to invite her new boyfriend over.

Our father loved nothing more than an audience. He got up, whistled a few bars of that old song about Daisy, Daisy and being half crazy for the love of you. Opened the fridge, returned to his seat with a bottle of beet juice, placed it in the center of the table.

I picked it up. "Seriously?"

"Good for what ails you," he said.

"I'll take your word for it," I said.

He grinned and drummed the table with his finger-tips. "So there I was. Boxes to the left of me. Boxes to the right of me. I borrowed one of those dolly things from Mick, he's the UPS guy, and together we loaded up a case of dog food to donate to the Marshbury Animal Shelter."

He poured some beet juice, took a sip, cracked us up with the face he made. "Don't you worry now, I saved another whole case of pooch food for the grand-dogs. Anyhoo, I hightailed it down to the shelter just as the crew in charge of the joint was returning from their lunch break."

Carol checked the kitchen clock again.

"And while they were unloading the dog food from my trunk, who do you think pulled her car right into the spot next to mine?"

"Lassie?" I said.

"None other than Sweepstakes Sally, the reigning queen of her very own Sweeps Dream Team. She was dropping off three cases of kitty litter she'd won, though I talked her into hanging on to one bag and even offered to sprinkle it over her walkway when the first snow hits."

"Now *there's* a pickup line," Carol said.

I put my iced tea down with a clunk. "Wait. Is Sweepstakes Sally the same Sally we were supposed to meet today?"

Our dad wiggled his eyebrows. "The one and only."

"Great," Christine said.

Carol crossed her arms over her chest. "We don't care what else you do with her, Dad, but do *not*, under any circumstances, let her touch your credit cards."

Three

Lorna and Gloria, two of my favorite teachers at Bayberry Preschool, and I always got together for drinks near the end of the summer. It was a ritual that softened the jolt of all that free time screeching to a halt, and helped us ease our way gently toward another school year.

Lorna's car was off having a back-to-school tune-up, so I swung by to pick her up. Since we were meeting Gloria at Bayberry, I'd loaded up a cardboard box of stuff to drop off in my classroom.

Lorna was waiting outside when I pulled into her driveway, her own box of classroom supplies sitting on her front steps. I jumped out of my car and slid my stuff over on the backseat to make room for hers.

"Hey," I said.

By way of greeting, Lorna started checking out the provisions I'd packed. My father had managed to win three cases of disinfectant wipes. A disinfectant wipe is a teacher's best friend, so I'd commandeered my share immediately. I'd also staked my claim on some mini-Bundt pans that seemed to me to hold endless pre-school possibilities, and a few other things.

"Beet juice?" Lorna said as we both buckled up.

"My father won it," I said. "I don't know if it will fly at snack time, but we can always turn it into a science experiment."

"Right," Lorna said. "We can make everybody chug a paper cup full of beet juice and then we can time how long it takes for their pee to turn red."

"I can't believe they actually let you teach children," I said. "Unless you were referring to our colleagues. Perhaps our fearless leader could use it for a team building activity."

"Don't you dare suggest it," Lorna said. "That bitch of a boss of ours certainly doesn't need our help when it comes to torturing the teaching staff. Maybe we could use it for a tie-dye classroom activity. You know how nothing stains like beet juice. We could have each of the kids bring in a white T-shirt from home . . . Wait, your father didn't happen to win any carrot juice, did he? It would be a nice contrast. Maybe with a little spinach puree thrown in?"

"Right," I said, "and then we'll send the T-shirts home with the kids, and that night on the news they'll announce that spinach puree causes cancer. And we'll be up all night fielding irate phone calls from parents."

"I forget," Lorna said. "Is apple juice still bad, or did the pendulum swing and it's good again? Never mind, let's keep the suspense going right up until school starts. All I know is that I'm glad I had my own kids back when they practically ordered you to drink a dark beer while you breastfed."

We drove along the tree-lined streets of Marshbury. I hung a right off the main road and cruised up the long entrance drive to the school. We passed a totem pole made of brightly colored clay fish and a row of painted plywood cutouts of teddy bears. Boxwood sheared in the shape of ducks edged the walkway to the Cape Cod shingled building.

Back in the day, the school had purchased real sheep and goats and there'd been vague plans of preschool yarn spinning and knitting, even cheese-making. Coyotes put a tragic end to that dream, and the school went back to housing the occasional classroom guinea pig. Still, even without livestock, Bayberry Preschool was that perfect combination of artsy fartsy and immaculately groomed landscaping that kept the students happy while allowing their parents to justify the exorbitant tuition they paid.

I pulled into the TEACHER OF THE MONTH parking spot.

"Ha," Lorna said. "That's really funny."

"School hasn't started yet," I said. "We can park wherever the hell we want."

"Okay," Lorna said. "Here's the plan. We get in and get out fast. No hanging around like those kiss-butt teachers who waste half their summers here. We spend

way too much of our own time and money on this place
as it is. If Gloria hasn't shown up yet, we can always
text her from the bar and tell her to meet us there."

A sleek red sedan drove up and pulled into a space
marked PRINCIPAL. Even without that clue, I was
smart enough to know the car belonged to Kate Stone,
Bayberry Preschool's founding owner.

"Maybe not," I said. I put the key back into the igni-
tion, started up my Civic.

"Wimp," Lorna said as I backed out of TEACHER
OF THE MONTH and pulled into an unmarked
parking place.

Lorna gave our boss a big phony queen-like wave,
her hand twisting back and forth at the wrist. "Okay,
maybe we'll just hang around for a couple minutes,
stockpile a few brownie points."

. . . . .

I wouldn't admit it to many people, but the truth
was that just walking into my classroom usually gave
me a little thrill. Even now when most of the smaller
stuff was still packed away in boxes, stacked alongside
the larger items in the far corner, everything covered
with sheets of plastic. The windows had been washed,
the area rug steam cleaned, the empty shelves touched
up with a coat of fresh white paint.

By the end of the school year, the floor would be
dotted and spotted with preschool detritus. A
mysterious, overripe scent that nothing could touch
would tinge the air, just out of reach.

But right now my classroom was virginal, magical, filled with promise. And more than anywhere else, it was my place in the world.

Just to see how they'd look, I put the box on the floor and unpacked a few of the baby Bundt pans, spaced them evenly across the top of one of the low shelves. Maybe I'd put markers in one, blunt-tipped scissors in another, a handful of crayons in the third. Items that would be easy to dump out if I decided to wash the pans and use them for actual cooking.

Once the full list of this year's classroom allergies had come in via the school nurse, I'd see what ingredients were left to work with. As long as we left out the nuts, mini-pumpkin bread would make for a nice early autumn snack, and I was pretty sure it was a culinary adventure the full-day kids and I could pull off.

I put the beet juice away in the supply closet, then leaned over the box again to grab the wipes.

"Knock-knock," a male voice said behind me. I jumped, twisting my body around to a more dignified position. Why is it that in those rare unguarded moments when your butt is sticking out for the whole wide world to see—pulling weeds in your garden, unpacking classroom supplies—people invariably beep as they drive by or sneak up and say *knock-knock*?

A really good-looking guy—sun-bleached blondish hair, long belted shorts, V-neck T-shirt bursting with broad shoulders—stood just inside my doorway. He held out his hand, took a few steps toward me with a noticeable limp.

"Ethan Buchanan," he said. He had a deep voice with a hint of scratchiness to it, the perfect accompaniment to the stubble on his cheeks.

"Sarah Hurlihy," I said. "But I'm not officially even here, so pretend you didn't hear that." I smiled and gave his hand a quick shake, then stepped past him toward the door. This was not the first time a divorced or separated parent had tried to waylay me in the class-room before the school year had officially started. The details varied, but it was always about control—and making sure I knew that he, or she, was the good parent. I was a professional, so I'd deal with it. But not one summer minute sooner than I had to.

He laughed. "I'm not officially here yet either, but it's nice to meet you anyway. And once we're no longer figments and we're officially teachers, you can find me in the classroom right next door."

I looked at him. He smiled a sun-streaked smile.

"Wait," I said. "You can't be next door. That's Lorna's classroom."

. . . . .

I found Lorna leaning up against my car.

"I am so freakin' mad I am spitting bullets," she said. "Do you have any idea how many years I've been in that classroom? I practically raised the beams or the boards or whatever they are and built it with my own two hands. What kind of animal strolls into a brand new teaching job and steals a classroom from a senior teacher? What kind of administrator allows it to happen?"

"Maybe it's an accessibility thing," I said. "Your classroom is the closest one to the front door and he walks with a pretty big limp."

"Oh, puh-lease. He probably fell off his surfboard. Or he's faking the limp just to get his stinking mitts on my classroom."

Lorna turned around and kicked one of my tires.

"That's it," I said. "Let it all out. Just go easy on the tires—I need them to last until our first paycheck. Come on, let's get out of here and go have that drink."

Lorna crossed her arms over her chest. "First I'm going to march right in there and tell that bitch of a boss of ours to give me my freakin' classroom back."

I put my hand on her forearm. "You know, I think you should wait until you cool down. Let some time pass, make a few notes. Maybe work on your phrasing a little bit. You can call Kate Stone tomorrow and set up an appointment to talk to her. We can rehearse what you'll say before you go."

The front door opened and we both turned to look. Gloria, one of our favorite colleagues and partners in crime, gave us a big wave. She crossed the parking lot in her long lanky stride, half skip, half gallop.

"Ohmigod," she said. "Did you check out that new teacher? Now that's what I call one helluva hunk of man. Hunk, hunk, H-U-N-K, hunk."

"The preschool teacher hunk bar is not necessarily the highest," I said, mostly to soften the blow for Lorna.

"He's not that hunky," Lorna said. "And he stole my freakin' classroom."

"Oh, sweetie," Gloria said. "What a shame. But I know you, you'll make your next classroom even more amazing. And just think, you can spend the first half of the year pretending you thought you'd left something behind so you can get some flirt time in with the new school hunk."

Lorna and I stared at Gloria.

"What the hell happened to your hair?" Lorna said.

Four

Gloria took a sip of her Lemon Drop martini. "So. Tell me the truth. Do you hate it?"

I'm old enough to know that when a friend says *tell me the truth*, she doesn't usually mean it. What she really wants you to do is tell her what she's hoping to hear. I might have been guilty of setting this kind of friendship trap a time or two myself over the years.

I kept my nose buried in my own Lemon Drop martini.

Lorna swallowed and put her martini glass down. "I love it. It's just what the doctor ordered. Still summery, but with a kick. What's in it again, Sarah?"

I took another sip as I considered Lorna's decoy question. I was actually pretty good with ingredients as long as I didn't have to cook them. I counted them off on my fingers. "Vodka, lemon juice, sugar, possibly even superfine—"

"We put triple sec in ours," our waitress said as she approached our booth. "Watch out for the places that sneak sweet and sour mix in there. Nasty stuff."

"Thanks for the warning," Lorna said. "We'll be careful."

Our waitress nodded, her mission to protect us from sweet and sour mix accomplished. "Can I get you another round, ladies?"

Lorna nodded. "Thanks," I said. Gloria stared straight ahead.

I reached for a pita triangle and dunked it in the spinach and kale dip.

"You both know I'm not talking about the Lemon Drops," Gloria said. "My hair. You hate it."

"No we don't hate it," Lorna said. She reached for her own pita triangle. "Exactly."

I gave Lorna a knock-it-off look. "I think it might be that it's just so different. It could be taking us some time to get used to it because we've known you for so long with your other hair."

Gloria closed her eyes. "I knew it wasn't good. My husband has been calling me Susie Straight Hair and my youngest screamed when he first saw it. I guess I just thought it would look more like the hair in the infomercials."

"Relax," I said. "As soon as you wash it, you'll be your old self again."

Gloria shook her head. Her hair waited a moment, then followed limply.

"How long is it supposed to last?" Lorna asked.

Gloria drained her first Lemon Drop, looked around for our waitress. "Forever? At least it cost enough to last forever."

I gave her hair a closer inspection. Her usual medium brown hair had the texture of a Brillo pad. This new hair looked longer straight. It was shinier. It kind of hung together as one piece, like a curtain of hair. It turned upward at the ends just a tiny bit, not quite a curl. More like a dent.

"I know," I said. "It's a little bit like Marlo Thomas's hair in *That Girl.*"

Gloria's face lit up. "That's good, right?"

"Sure, maybe if this was 1969," Lorna said.

"Don't listen to her," I said. "It's not even close to a hair disaster. Once when I was seven or eight, my sister Carol got about a dozen of those pink curlers with the hard plastic teeth stuck in my hair, and my mother had to cut them out. Now *that* was a hair disaster."

I gave Lorna a jump-in-any-time look.

"My friends and I used to iron ours," Lorna said. "We'd fan our hair out over the ironing board, and then somebody else would put a towel over it and iron it."

"You were supposed to use a towel?" I said. "Boyohboy, I wish I'd known that. I can still smell scorched hair just thinking about it."

"I used my father's hot comb, too," Lorna said. "Remember those? Like an early version of a curling iron, but it was supposed to straighten instead. All it really did was make my hair reek of Brylcreem."

"Brylcreem, a little dab'll do ya," I sang. I didn't get the melody quite right, but in my defense it was a pretty ancient commercial. "Oh, and my friends and I used to roll our hair around orange juice cans at pajama parties. Have you ever tried sleeping on a head full of orange juice cans? I'm pretty sure all that metal helped us pick up some extra radio stations though."

We all reached for our new drinks.

"Good job," Gloria said to us as our waitress walked away. "I think I almost feel better now."

"Great," Lorna said. "Okay, my turn. What the hell are the three of us going to do to get my classroom back?"

. . . . .

"So, how did it feel to be back at school?" John asked.

I'd put my cell on speakerphone to keep my neck from cramping, then switched it back because it felt more intimate to have him talking directly into my ear.

"Good," I said. I pulled the pillow out from behind my back and tucked it behind my head. "Well, mostly good, but there's always that end-of-summer tinge of dread. I'm not sure if it's a carryover from my own school days, or if it's more about all the unknowns of a new school year."

"But you'll keep most of the same students, right?"

"Yeah. Ideally, all the kids stay in the same classroom for three years, with an equal mix of first, second, and third-years. The third-year students stay for a full day, while the younger kids leave just before lunch."

"Lucky kids." I thought I could hear wistfulness in his voice. I wasn't sure whether it meant that he'd like to be a preschool student himself or that a part of him wished he had a kid he could send to preschool.

There was a beat of silence.

I switched the phone to my other ear, remembered it was my turn to talk. "I like to think so. The older kids help teach the younger kids, which reinforces their own skills, and having a smaller group in the afternoon gives me the time to make sure they'll be ready to hit the ground running in kindergarten. And they think they're hot stuff by the time they get to that last year, so it's great for their self-esteem, too. It's a good structure. Of course, the reality is that families move, or split up, or parents decide that attendance at a more prestigious preschool might up their offspring's chances to get into Harvard—"

"Instead of kindergarten?"

"Don't think I haven't been asked to write a recommendation or two."

He laughed.

"How are the Gamiacs doing?" I asked. John ran the accounting department for a Boston gaming and technology company called Necrogamiac, and earlier in the summer he'd managed to get me hired as a consultant to ramp up the social skills of some of the younger IT employees. I'd enjoyed working with them, and it had been a nice break from my usual stint at Bayberry summer camp in some ways. In other ways, the Gamiacs were like supersized preschoolers, so it really hadn't turned out to be that different after all.

"They ask about you every time I run into them in the hallway. I promised I'd talk you into coming back for a visit soon."

"Absolutely," I said. "You won't even have to twist my arm."

John Anderson and I were on a roll. We'd figured out a schedule of cross-cohabitation between my house in Marshbury and his condo in Boston, with some alone time thrown in for good measure. His puppy Horatio no longer hated my guts. The sex was good. We never ran out of things to talk about.

Sometimes I thought John and I might even spend the rest of our lives together. Unless, of course, I managed to screw things up.

I had a lifelong pattern of screwing things up with men. If I had to attribute this to any one thing in a veritable sea of choices, I'd probably have to go with my tendency to think that if said men had voluntarily chosen to be with me, something must be seriously wrong with them.

I was pretty sure I'd moved past John's questionable taste and had even come to think of it as clearly to my advantage. This might not put me at the top of the leaderboard of self-esteem, but in my own little corner it felt like growth.

Still, I had to admit a tiny part of me was a step re-moved, waiting to see how long this would last. Wondering what would eventually go wrong. How my heart would get broken this time around. How long it would take me to move on.

I knew how to move on to the next guy. But I really, really didn't want to do that anymore. What I wanted to figure out was how to stick around and make things work.

When John spoke, I'd almost forgotten we were still on the phone. "I'd say we have just enough time for a road trip before you get all caught up in another year of teaching."

I leaned back against my headboard. Pictured John leaning back against his. Thought for a moment that maybe my marriage to Kevin might have lasted if we'd kept separate places, the yin of togetherness balanced by the yang of being apart. Ruled that out as I realized the yin/yang thing would have probably only made Kevin screw around on me sooner rather than later.

"Sounds like fun," I said. "Where do you think we should go?"

"How about we both put on our thinking caps, and when we see each other tomorrow night, we'll make a decision."

I smiled. I loved that John said dorky things like *thinking caps*. It was part of his charm.

"Tomorrow night's my house, right?" I jumped out of bed and headed for my office, where I'd tacked our schedule on the bulletin board over my desk.

"I think so," John said. "Wait, let me pull up my calendar. Yep, your house. Whoa, the dog days of summer are dwindling fast."

On John's side of the phone, Horatio let out a bark.

"Ooh, he knows his tribe already," I said. "That's pretty advanced for a puppy. You might want to start thinking Ivy League."

"I'm on it. I've been doing puppy genius flashcards with him twice a day for an hour."

"Ha," I said. "Wait, you *are* kidding, right?"

Five

John was making a zucchini-crusted pizza, something I'd never even known was an epicurean possibility, while I walked Horatio around my neighborhood. Mellow was my goal, and mellow did not come easily to Horatio, whose mother was a Yorkie with a bad attitude who lived in John's building. Said mother was assumed to have briefly crossed paths with a runaway greyhound, both weeks short of being spayed and neutered respectively. Even though Horatio somehow came out looking more like a scruffy dachshund, he had definitely inherited his mother's predisposition to high energy.

As a preschool teacher, I knew high energy well. Kids need to move, and sadly, they often don't get enough movement either at home or at school. There's also this crazy misperception that if you get kids all wound up, you won't be able to reel them back in. The truth is that a well-exercised child is a well-behaved child.

When students are having a hard time sitting still in my classroom, I build in extra movement for them. I also suggest that their mothers or fathers or nannies stop by the nearest track so they can do a few laps on the way to school. Or make them jump up and down fifty times in the driveway before they jump into the car. Or start the day with a family dance party. The kids and I like to begin our mornings with Raffi's oldie but goodie, "Shaking our Sillies Out." I figured if the walk didn't work out, I could always hum a few bars for Horatio.

I picked up the pace. Horatio tried to get ahead of me, so I gave the leash a quick correction.

Horatio heeled. "What a good boy," I said. Positive reinforcement is another one of my magic teacher tricks.

Per John's suggestion, I'd had my thinking cap on all day. I'd even scrolled through some last-minute vacation sites online. There were lots of deals that would be perfect for an end-of-summer getaway. As far as I was concerned, John and I could just do eeny-meeny-miny-mo. Anywhere with a beach and a bed would be fine by me.

When Horatio and I turned the corner, my father's sea green Mini Cooper was just pulling into my drive-way. Since the phrase *call first* was apparently not in my family's vocabulary, my only hope for an uninterrupted pizza date with John was to head him off at the driveway.

I picked up my pace as the car door swung open. My father heaved himself out of the driver's seat. He adjusted his driving cap to a jauntier angle and gave me a cross between a wave and a salute. Horatio barked.

"Dad," I said. "Thanks for stopping by, but—"

"Thanks for asking, honey, but we've already got dinner plans. Sally just wanted to stop by and meet you."

He walked around to the passenger side and opened the door. The door closed again, so quickly I thought I might have imagined it opening at all.

My father crossed the space between us in three long steps and kissed me on the cheek. "Sarah, my darlin' daughter. Don't you look as lovely as the day is long." He bent down to pat Horatio. Horatio's tail started wagging a mile a minute.

"Thanks, Dad." I eyed the Mini Cooper. From this angle I couldn't be sure anyone was inside. An imaginary girlfriend would certainly be a new twist, even for my father.

He swung his arm around my shoulder and steered Horatio and me over to his car. A woman was texting away in the passenger seat. We waited a moment. My dad tapped the window politely. The window rolled down.

"Hi," I said. "I'm Sarah. You must be Sally."

She held up a manicured index finger, went back to texting.

I leaned forward to get a good look. It was hard to tell how old she was. Her fine hair had been highlighted so many times that the ends appeared to disintegrate as opposed to just ending. She wore a crisp white blouse with the collar turned up. I could just see the pointy toes of her fancy shoes poking out from under tight jeans. Several chunky rings and an overabundance of bracelets vaguely coordinated with her gold-edged cell phone cover.

I hated her already.

"Give her a minute," my father said, as if either of us had a choice in the matter. "Oh, wait, I've got a box in the back for you. Sidewalk chalk in twelve assorted colors or some such thing."

"You won a case of sidewalk chalk? Way to go, Dad. My students will be all over it."

"Just sharing the spoils, kiddo, just sharing the spoils."

My father opened the hatchback and I leaned in to grab the box. Horatio jumped up, hoping for treats.

"Watch the paint job, young fellow," my father said.

"Billy?" A voice said from the car. The door opened and Sally stepped out.

"See?" my father said. "What'd I tell you? She's dying to meet you."

Sally glanced up from her phone. Her sun-damaged neck made me think of a snakeskin purse. Her face didn't match her neck—it had a puffy, doll-like quality to it, and her upper lip was particularly swollen, as if a bee had stung it. I resisted the urge to offer her some Benadryl.

"Hello there," she said.

"Hey," I said.

She dropped her head. Her thumbs danced on her phone. "Listen, Billy," she said without looking up. "We have to fly so we can make the Sweeps Dream Team meeting on time."

"So, we'll arrive fashionably late," my father said. "The better to make a grand entrance."

Her thumbs never stopped. "It's at your house. I switched it."

"What?" I said. Horatio crouched low and growled in Sally's direction. I resisted the urge to join him.

"Then they'll just have to make themselves at home till we get there," my father said, "won't they now?"

I shifted the box of sidewalk chalk in my arms. Horatio looked up at me.

"*Now*, Billy. We've got a big win waiting for us just around the corner—I can feel it." Without further ado, my father's new girlfriend texted her way back to the car and climbed in.

"Well," my father said. "You can't argue with that, now can you?"

"Dad?" was all I could come up with.

His car actually beeped. He leaned over, kissed me on top of my head, patted Horatio on top of his.

"Lovely to meet me," I said to my father's disappearing Mini Cooper. "The pleasure was all yours."

. . . . .

"Sit," I said.

Horatio sat. I unhooked his leash. He made a beeline for the kitchen.

When I caught up to him, his rear end was going a mile a minute and he was slobbering all over John's face.

"How'd it go?" John asked.

I pushed my father and his new girlfriend out of my head. Having a big family is great, but they have a tendency to suck all the extra air out of your life if you let them. The trick is to set limits. I'd call Carol later so she could figure out what to do. In the meantime, I'd focus on my own little corner of the world.

I flashed John a big smile. "Great. Horatio is a well-behaved and truly gifted walker."

John managed to peel Horatio off him so he could stand up again and pull me in for a kiss. Horatio let out a soft whine. Not long ago, he would have tried to take me out, so this was major progress.

John popped the zucchini crusted pizza into the oven, and we adjourned to my tiny dining room. The table was set. The candles were lit. The wine was poured.

"Wow," I said. "I might have to keep you around for a while."

John held my chair for me, then put a bone-shaped treat on the floor for Horatio.

Finally he took his own seat and raised his glass. "To us."

"To us."

We sipped our wine without taking our eyes off each other. I was just about to suggest we pause the pizza and finish cooking it later, much later.

"Okay, you first," John said. "What did you come up with for road trip ideas?"

"Well," I said. "Let me put my thinking cap back on first." I mimed putting on a hat and tying an imaginary bow under my chin.

John smiled.

"Okay, that's better. Let's see. Well, the Vineyard and Nantucket will be mob scenes, and I doubt we could still get hotel reservations anyway. Same with the Cape and pretty much the whole New England coast, even if we head north instead of south."

John nodded.

"So I bookmarked some last-minute vacation sites. I was thinking we could just pick somewhere that's off season, or a little bit off the beaten path. Honestly, it doesn't matter to me where we go, as long as we get to have an adventure together."

"I feel that way, too." John reached out and put his hand on mine, touching off one of those great high voltage sparks of electricity between us.

The buzzer went off on my stove, as if we'd triggered it. John pushed his chair back and stood up.

"I think I've found the perfect place," he said. "Lift up your plate. And let me know what you think."

I lifted my plate. Tucked under it was a computer printout perfectly folded up like a brochure.

Camp Winnabone.
A Ruff and Ready Happy Camper Canine Camp.
Featuring Our Famous Daily Yappy Hour.

. . . . .

When John came back with the pizza, I was still carefully considering my response. John was a pretty straightforward kind of guy, so I didn't think this was a test. But, still, to say he was attached to Horatio was an understatement at least the size of Texas.

In terms of geography, it truly didn't matter to me where John and I went on our road trip. But I had to admit that my romantic fantasies were decidedly puppy-less. And they definitely did not include making love to the accompaniment of soft puppy whining from the other side of the door. Or getting up in the middle of the night and scavenging for enough clothes to avoid getting arrested for indecent exposure during a puppy pee excursion. Or waking up to hit the bathroom myself only to step on puppy poop or puppy puke halfway to my destination.

Horatio loved going to his puppy play care, which also did overnight boarding, so there was absolutely no reason to feel guilty about leaving him while we went away for a quick trip. He probably wouldn't even miss us.

"Let's eat," I said, "before the pizza gets cold."

The zucchini crusted pizza was amazing, almost like a frittata and bursting with end-of-summer freshness. A sexy breeze blew in through my open dining room windows. I took another sip of the white wine John had brought with him. I chewed another bite of pizza.

His treat finished, Horatio skidded across the hardwood floor and crashed head first into one leg of the table. I grabbed my wineglass fast.

John scooped up Horatio, checked him for boo-boos, dragged his bed from the living room into the dining room, got him settled in with his favorite stuffed squirrel. He passed by me on his way back to his seat and picked up the brochure.

"Mmm, this is delish," I said. On some level, I knew it was true. Even if I was having a hard time actually tasting it because visions of canine camp were dancing in my head, blocking out pretty much everything else.

John took a healthy bite, closed his eyes while he chewed and swallowed. "Not bad. The trick is to salt the zucchini after you shred it, let it sit, and then squeeze out all the extra liquid so the crust doesn't get soggy."

"Who knew," I said.

I gulped some wine. With preschoolers, redirection is relatively straightforward. For example, say one of my students does something annoying, like jumping up and down on another student. I simply scoop him up and say, "It's not okay to jump on Pandora, Gulliver." Then, while my assistant is checking Pandora for serious injuries, I take Gulliver to another part of the classroom. Together we outline a little circle of personal jumping space with plastic tape. And then I say to Gulliver, "When you need to jump, it's okay to do it right here, as long as you're all by yourself in your own little circle."

I knew there had to be a similar way to redirect John from canine camp to, say, an all-inclusive in the Dominican Republic, but I couldn't quite wrap my head around it.

John put his wine glass down and picked up the folded paper. "A destination experience for canines and their humans. Private cabins with fully enclosed doggie yards. Fully drinkable fountains with triple-filtered water. Private meditation gardens. Over one hundred and sixty acres of untouched nature to roam. Choice of thirty-two land and lake activities each day. Daily yappy hour. Campfire howl alongs. Agility training. Skateboarding. Square dancing. Buff, fluff and puff spa treatments. Pawdicures. "

"Did you hear that, buddy?" John said. I was pretty sure he was talking to Horatio and not me.

"Campfire howl alongs?" I said. "Really?"

"I know, how great is that? I wonder if we'll get to make s'mores, although maybe not, since chocolate is one of the most common causes of canine poisoning."

"Right," I said. "How fair would it be if only the people got to eat the s'mores? It's not like the dogs wouldn't be sharing *their* treats."

John sighed. "I always wanted to go to sleepover camp when I was a kid, but my parents never let me. It might sound crazy, but this is kind of a dream come true for me."

I gulped some wine, resisted the urge to reach for the bottle.

John was still talking. "Listen, how about if I give the camp a call after dinner and see if they've got room for us the week after next? I'll MapQuest it to double-check, but I'm pretty sure it's only about a four or five-hour drive from Marshbury. Beautiful country out that way."

John's Heath Bar eyes held mine. His eyes were his best feature, a ring of chocolate brown around a smaller circle of toffee.

I dug deep for my happy camper smile.

John tilted his head. "Unless you'd rather do something else?"

Six

"What could I say? I mean, John was crazy excited about going and I didn't want to ruin it for him."

Lorna put on her blinker. "So, what's the problem? You drop off the mutt at archery or his sit-upon making class, then the two of you head back to your cabin for forty-two uninterrupted minutes of hot sex in your private meditation garden before you have to pick him up again."

I sighed. "Yeah, I guess." Lorna referred to her husband as Mattress Man, and her biggest hope for their marriage seemed to be to get him to occasionally put down the television remote and climb out of bed. I wasn't sure Lorna and I necessarily agreed on the definition of *problem*.

"Okay, enough about you," Lorna said. "Help me rehearse what I'm going to say one more time."

As we drove up the hill to Bayberry Preschool, a landscaper in work boots and a green felt beret was trimming the boxwood ducks. I quacked.

"Come on," Lorna said. "This is serious. Focus."

"All right, I'm Kate Stone and you've just knocked. I open my office door and you say . . ."

"Bitch."

"Probably not your best opening line. Whatever she's wearing, tell her she looks great, or you love that color on her."

"She's been rotating the same six batik tunics since 1993. And they're all either the color of berries or dog poop."

At the top of the hill, we took a right into the parking lot. Kate Stone, wearing a cranberry batik tunic, was just getting out of her car.

"Duck," Lorna said.

It took me a moment to realize she was talking to me and not belatedly pointing out one of the boxwood topiaries we'd just passed. I ducked. Lorna pulled into a space at the far end of the parking lot.

"I can't believe you made me do that." I sat up, fluffed my hair.

"I don't want that bitch of a boss of ours to think we're in cahoots. Listen, stay here until I'm inside, then count to ten. And don't forget to lock my car. And whatever you do, don't lose my keys. And make sure you walk around and go in the back door. "

"Did you really just say *in cahoots?*"

"Ohmigod," Lorna whispered. "Don't look."

I angled Lorna's rear view mirror so I could look.

Lorna pulled the mirror in her direction. I pulled it back, splitting the distance between us so we could both see.

Ethan, the new teacher, was just climbing out of the passenger side of Kate Stone's car.

"They must have had a breakfast meeting," I said. "Or maybe she picked him up hitchhiking or something."

Kate Stone emerged and leaned back against her shiny red sedan. Ethan walked around to her side of the car. He reached out and touched her hair, so quickly it was almost as if it hadn't happened.

"She probably just had a piece of leaf stuck in her hair," I said. "Or lint."

Our boss threw her head back and laughed. Ethan joined in, then reached to take an overstuffed shopping bag from her. She pulled the bag away. He grinned and pulled back. She gave in and handed it over. They walked toward the main entrance of the school, their arms so close they were practically touching, Ethan's limp creating a rhythm of its own.

"So now we know how he got my classroom," Lorna said.

"We don't know anything."

"Sure we do. They are absolutely, one hundred percent screwing around together. Either that or they're about to."

I couldn't take my eyes off them. "I don't think one hundred percent works in either/or situations."

Ethan shifted the bag to one arm, opened the door with his free hand and held it for Kate Stone. She stopped, one foot on the threshold. Turned her head toward him and smiled, her face inches from his.

"Holy guacamole," I said. "I think you might be one hundred percent right."

. . . . .

When I got to my classroom, my assistant June was sitting cross-legged in the middle of the floor. June was hard working and sweet, and the kids loved her. She was also ridiculously young and beautiful, with china doll blue eyes and shimmery blond hair that reached almost to her waist. I must have been feeling uncharacteristically self-confident when I'd chosen her from a large pool of applicants. As I remembered, I'd been particularly impressed by her professed high tolerance for dealing with the many and varied bodily fluids of preschoolers, vital in a teaching assistant.

June had turned out to be a great choice. Her only real flaw, other than her youth and her looks, was that she could fall into deep meditation at the drop of a juice box. One minute I'd see her wiping down the white board or helping a child with a wooden puzzle, and the next minute she was gone. I'd find her in the reading corner or on the floor in the storage area. Eyes closed, palms up, index fingers and thumbs touching.

I had to admit this was better than having an assistant who disappeared to smoke a cigarette or even crack. Still, the next time I needed to hire an assistant,

I'd know enough to ask: *Do you spend inordinate amounts of time meditating when you should be scrubbing Play-Doh off tabletops?*

"Hey," I said.

June looked up. "I thought I'd get the circle taped down." She held up a roll of orange tape and our teacher scissors.

The circle is the heart of the classroom, an implied group hug. It provides togetherness. It brings order and a sense of security, limits as well as predictability. It becomes a theater-in-the-round for singing, sharing, stories, games, activities.

But even when you use the most overpriced specialty floor-marking tape available to make it, a classroom circle is pretty much toast by the end of a school year. If you're lucky enough that it lasts that long. At which point somebody has to make a fresh one. And I was seriously circle-challenged.

A classroom circle has to be a true circle—not an oval, or an ellipse, or a rectangle, or a triangle—so that everybody has full view of everybody else when they're sitting on it. It has to be big enough for each child to stand up and swing his or her arms without taking out another student.

I could always picture my classroom circle so clearly. I knew the perfect location. I could see myself drawing it with chalk and then stretching the plastic tape gently until it morphed into just the right curve. But despite my 20/20 circle vision, within moments of beginning to make it, the tape would have taken on a life of its own. It would stick to my hands, or to itself, or refuse to stick at all. And I'd be mumbling words under my breath that are not okay for a preschool teacher.

June was a genius at circles. I gave her a big smile. "Thanks. Next year I'll be all over it."

She shrugged, went back to work. I put my father's sidewalk chalk swag down on the floor next to the other boxes. I was just trying to decide whether to attempt to actually accomplish something or head for the teachers' room to grab a cup of coffee while I waited for Lorna, when my phone rang.

I stepped out into the hallway. "What's wrong?"

"Why does something have to be wrong?" my sister Carol said.

"Because you never call me unless you need something?"

Carol juggled her job as an event planner, four kids between the ages of almost three and seventeen, and a husband who traveled. She ran a tight ship, but if one little thing went wrong, the ripple effect was huge. Our sister Christine was usually her first call, but I was backup, especially during the summer months.

"Fine," she said. "Can you take Maeve for a little while this afternoon? The boys are at soccer camp and I've got to get to the office for a couple of hours and Siobhan can't—"

"Why can't Christine do it?" Carol and Christine's youngest kids had been born a month apart. Even though they weren't technically Irish twins since they had different mothers, they spent so much time together they might as well have been.

Carol let out a puff of air. "Because Maeve tried to flush Sydney's doll down the toilet yesterday and called her a poophole."

"Wow, that's really advanced. Have you thought about having her tested?"

"Not funny."

"Maybe she wasn't calling Sydney a poophole. Maybe she was calling the toilet a poophole. Which, if you think about it, is pretty high level for a not-quite-three-year-old."

"Tell that to Christine. She thinks Maeve has officially scarred Sydney for life."

"Oh, puh-lease. Sydney has an older brother to do that. And we both know Christine was born overreacting. Remember when Johnny and Billy put a toad in her bed?"

Carol burst out laughing. "And she didn't stop hiccupping for, like, five days."

"And then she spent another five weeks trying to convince us post-traumatic hiccup syndrome was a real thing. She was such a little poophole."

In our family, it was perfectly acceptable to make fun of our siblings to their faces, but we were not supposed to do it behind their backs. The truth was we did it fairly often, though because we'd been raised Catholic, at least we had the good grace to feel guilty about it.

"But she's hardly ever a poophole anymore," I said to burn off some guilt.

"She was when I just called her," Carol said. "So, can I drop off Maeve around two?"

I walked over to the doorway of my classroom, peeked in to check the clock. June had disappeared, leaving a perfectly taped orange floor circle in her wake.

"Sure," I said. "And when you pick her up again, we can figure out what we're going to do about Dad."

"Maeve!" Carol screamed.

I was just coming to the definitive conclusion that Carol had hung up on me, when Ethan came out of Lorna's former classroom. He smiled at me. I smiled back, cellphone still to my ear. He limped by me and into my classroom.

"Make yourself at home," I mumbled. I pulled my cell away from my ear, crossed my arms over my chest, waited for him to realize he was lost and come back out. Stood there in the hallway for a moment. Decided it was ridiculous to stand there and followed him in.

"Just getting an early start on setting up my classroom," I said as I stepped through the doorway. I mean, in case he really was sleeping with the boss, it couldn't hurt to come across as a workaholic.

June jumped, blushed, stepped away from Ethan, whose arm seemed to have been around her. Or almost around her.

"Circle's done," she said as she yanked her tank top down over her yoga pants.

We looked at each other.

"Bye," she said.

Single file, they walked past me and disappeared into the hallway. I took a slow lap around my new classroom circle, rehearsing the lecture I'd give June the next time I saw her. About how it was never a good idea to mix business with pleasure, particularly if said pleasure was one hundred percent quite possibly already sleeping with one's boss.

Seven

"Where the hell did you disappear to with my keys?" Lorna said when I found her in the parking lot. "Do you know how embarrassing it is to have to hover like this?"

I dug for her keys and tossed them at her, possibly a bit harder than necessary. "You were supposed to call me on my cell when you were ready to leave."

Lorna clicked the car doors open. "Right, it was my fault. Apparently it always is."

"Meeting went well, huh?" I said as I climbed in and reached for my seatbelt.

"I. Don't. Want. To talk about it."

"Fine. Be. Like. That."

Lorna reached for her seatbelt. Once she was safely belted in, she pounded the steering wheel, alternating fists like a toddler pulverizing a rhythm instrument.

I sighed. "Listen. I know it doesn't feel like that right now, but it's only a classroom. The important thing is that you stood up to our bitch of a boss, and even if she didn't give your classroom back to you, on some level I'm sure she respects you for being assertive. It's not right that she took it away from you, but I think you need to rise above it. Focus on making your next classroom so incredible that everyone—Kate Stone, the new teacher, the other teachers—will know that it's not about four walls and a paint job."

Lorna assaulted the steering wheel some more. "And location—I could go from car to classroom in under a minute, which really comes in handy on those February mornings when you can't get out of bed. And let's not forget about the view—that room has the perfect tree for a bird feeder. Right outside the window."

"It doesn't matter. You're the magic, Lorna, not the location or the view. And you'll bring that magic with you to any classroom you have." I reached over and patted her knee. "Listen, it's a beautiful summery day, so let's forget all about this place and go have lunch."

My phone rang. I reached for it, just in case Carol was calling to say she didn't need me to watch Maeve after all.

The Bayberry Preschool number looked up from the screen. Maybe June had received my stay-away-from-the-new-teacher lecture telepathically and was calling to tell me she'd seen the light.

"Hello?" I said.

"Can you come in to my office?" Kate Stone's voice said.

I hunkered down in my seat. A summons from my boss always made me sure I'd done something wrong, as if being called to the principal's office could never be a good thing, no matter how old you got.

"Of course," I said in my best faux cheerful voice. "Let's see, I'll be in town later this week . . ."

"I meant now."

"Now? Well, actually, I was just in the middle of . . ." What, touring Prague? Climbing Mount Everest? Reading up on all the late-breaking preschool methodology? I looked through the windshield for inspiration.

My boss waved at me through her office window.

I waved back. "Now would be perfect."

"Great," Lorna said. "Now she definitely knows we're in cahoots."

. . . . .

Kate Stone's desk was made from a massive freeform slab of redwood. Whenever I saw it, I imagined a long-ago chain gang of Bayberry teachers cutting down the entire tree with tiny preschool scissors during a hell-on-earth inservice program that would only end when they finally yelled *Timber!*

The top of the desk had been polyurethaned until it was so shiny you could see how nervous you looked in the reflection. Which might well have been the point. I sat down, slid my chair a little closer to the desk, but not so close that my favorite summer T-shirt would get snagged on the rough bark that still edged it.

I looked up. I faked a smile. "That color is great on you," I lied. Pathetic.

My boss pushed up the sleeves of her cranberry batik tunic, rested her elbows on the desk, laced her fingers together. "Let's get right to the point. I think your assistant would be a good match for our new teacher."

It was such a bizarre thing to say that I couldn't quite wrap my brain around it. Kate Stone was soooo not the matchmaking type. Or the generous type. Or the type who would be okay with interstaff dating. And what about her own stomach-turning public display of affection with *our new teacher* that I'd witnessed earlier?

"You do?" was the best I could come up with.

"I do." She brushed her hands back and forth once, punctuation for a done deal, and reached for a pile of papers on her desk. "I've vetted the resumes on file and narrowed the choices down to the three most promising. You'll meet with them this week, preferably on Thursday, which will give me two days to get them in for a preliminary interview. Then you and I will reconvene and confirm our decision."

It took me a moment to realize that she was handing me the papers. I took them, then moved on to trying to figure out what this all had to do with June dating the new teacher.

"Wait," I said. "Are you telling me you want June to *work* with the new teacher?"

Kate Stone reached for her desktop Magic Eight Ball and turned it over with an obnoxious flourish. "All signs point to yes," she read. Or pretended to read. I didn't trust her for a second.

"But she's *my* assistant," I said. "I spent an entire year training her—"

"And now she'll be the perfect match for our new teacher, ensuring the continuity across the classrooms that Bayberry families have come to expect from us. And also fitting in nicely with my goal this year, Sarah, which is to keep the entire staff on their toes. Metaphorically, of course. Although perhaps I'll consider scheduling a ballet class for our first inservice to bring home the point in a more literal way as well."

"But . . ." Already June's perceived value was growing, like an old boyfriend whose faults faded more with each passing year. June was sweet and conscientious and industrious. She almost never took a sick day. The kids were crazy about her. Even when she disappeared to meditate, she always came back.

I cleared my throat. "I'm completely onboard for anything that's good for the school, of course. But I don't think June is ready for a switch. Even though she's come a long way, she still needs my guidance. And I think a new classroom situation might be, well, not in the best interests of the Bayberry community. Or continuity. Or even impunity."

I'd always thought the ability to rhyme on your feet was one of the marks of a good preschool teacher, but

Kate Stone didn't even bother to glance up. *Concentrate and ask again,* I imagined her Magic Eight Ball signaling me across the mammoth desk.

I concentrated. I put on my most dazzling smile. "How about this: June spends one more year under my supervision, with the goal being to get her up on her toes and ready to dance her way to another classroom next year?"

"Your assistant and I agree that she's ready to dance now."

"Wait," I said. "Are you telling me this was June's idea?"

My boss shook the Magic Eight Ball once more. "It has already been decided."

. . . . .

"Drive," I said before I was all the way into Lorna's car.

Lorna looked up from her phone. "Drive, please."

"Don't mess with me," I said.

"Got it." Lorna started her car and reached for her seatbelt. "Shall we find the nearest time zone where it's late enough to drink our lunch or should we just pretend we're in London?"

"It's beyond alcohol." I thunked my head back against the seat and closed my eyes. "Chocolate. Now."

We didn't say another word to each other until we were sitting on the steps of the bandstand looking out over the inner harbor. The ocean sparkled in the late summer sunlight, carefree and happy. I knew this meant that the stormy weather was all in my head, but it didn't make the roiling and churning I was feeling any less menacing.

Instead of chowing down to reach chocolate sedation level as soon as possible, I forced myself to take slow licks of my double-scoop Rocky Road. The last thing I needed right now was an ice cream headache on top of everything else.

"It's not that bad," Lorna said when I finished telling her. "Listen. I know it doesn't feel like it right now, but it's only an assistant. The important thing is that you stood up to our bitch of a boss, and even if she didn't give June back to you, I'm sure she respects you for being assertive. It's not right that she took her away from you, but I think you need to rise above it."

"I hate you," I said.

"You're the magic, Sarah, not June. And you'll bring that magic to any assistant you get stuck with this close to the start of the school year when we both know all the good ones have already been hired." She reached over and patted my knee.

"Point taken," I said. "But I still hate your guts. And get your hand off my knee."

We lapped in silence. I took a deep breath of salt air. It was a nice accompaniment to the ice cream, almost like sea-salted chocolate. I wondered if that's how somebody had come up with the idea, sitting at the edge of the ocean, devouring an ice cream cone. If I paid attention to things like that, maybe I could be a trendsetter, an entrepreneur, a chocolatier, instead of a preschool teacher. Maybe it was time to get out from under the clutches of my bitch of a boss and on to a new chapter of my life.

Lorna tucked some hair behind her ears to keep it out of the ice cream. "So, how do you think June will take it when you tell her?"

My eyes filled with tears. I tilted my head back and tried to blink them away before Lorna noticed.

"Kate Stone told me June already knows. And I think it might even have been her idea." I took a raggedy breath. "After all I've done for her."

Lorna didn't say anything.

"And he, *Ethan*, walked right into my classroom like he owned the place. And when I finally followed him in, I'm not one hundred percent sure but I think I walked in on some distinctly unteacherly behavior going on between the two of them. Ethan and June."

Most people might not realize this, but behind its innocent little facade, a preschool is a petri dish of drama and innuendo. Rumors grow and spread with the virulence of strep. I wondered if this was unique to preschools or if it was true about any workplace containing more than two people. Maybe gossip and speculation simply help pass the time between paychecks.

Lorna licked her ice cream cone while she considered. "Well, I have to say all signs point to an interesting year. But if you'd rather start our own pre-school and drive Bayberry out of business, I'd be up for that, too. We could scrawl graffiti all over everybody's white boards on our way out. In permanent marker. We just have to make sure we pack up every single thing we bought with our own money and take it with us."

I nodded. "Don't let me forget the sidewalk chalk and wipes my dad just won. I think I'll leave the beet juice though, since I have more at home. Or maybe we can use the beet juice to make water balloons and throw them over our shoulders on our way out."

Lorna sighed. "Setting up our own school would be a lot of work. The parents have already signed their contracts and put down deposits. And paid at least the first month's tuition by now, too. Maybe we could do something else for the first half of the school year, and then steal all the Bayberry students in January."

I considered this. "We've signed our contracts, too, so we'd have to figure out how to get fired."

"Like that would be hard."

I swallowed the last crunchy bite of ice cream cone and chased it down with a breath of salt air. "How about we both ponder the possibilities. And then we can reconvene over chocolate and make our final decision."

Eight

Carol beeped twice in my driveway.

"Mommy's here," I said to Maeve.

"Mommy is a poophole," Maeve pronounced. Since my niece had arrived, she'd used her new favorite word approximately forty-two times.

Both Carol and Christine planned to enroll their youngest kids at Bayberry next year once they were old enough, requesting me as the teacher. Of course, this would only fly if my boss didn't catch wind that they were my nieces. In a town the size of Marshbury, the chances of pulling this off were slim to none, but up until a couple of hours ago I'd been completely onboard.

Now I wasn't so sure. A word like poophole could spread through a preschool class faster than a runny nose. When the new word emerged on the car ride home, or at the dinner table, my phone would be ringing off the hook.

I wiggled my Sleeping Beauty finger puppet at Maeve. "Mommy is a beautiful princess."

Maeve wiggled the Cruella de Ville finger puppet she'd chosen back at me. "Mommy is a poophole."

"Okay then," I said. "Let's not keep the poophole waiting." I pulled off my finger puppet and tossed it back into the puppet box I'd borrowed from Bayberry, then scooped up my niece. She yanked Cruella off her finger and lobbed her right into the box. Superior hand/eye coordination might be another red flag for having Maeve in my class. As a teacher, you spent a lot less time mopping up bloody noses when you had students whose aim wasn't quite there yet.

"Auntie Sarah says you a poophole," Maeve greeted her mother when we got out to her minivan.

Carol peered over the top of her sunglasses at me.

"Don't look at me," I said. "I didn't teach it to her."

Carol pushed the button that slid open the side door of her minivan and jumped out. I handed Maeve over, and Carol had her buckled into her car seat before I'd managed to get my seatbelt on."

"You're so efficient," I said.

Carole clicked her own seatbelt into place. "Practice. Too much damn practice."

"Damn," Maeve said behind us. "Damn, damn, damn. Damn!"

. . . . .

I gave the tarnished brass doorknocker the obligatory thunk before I opened the door. "Da-ad," I yelled.

Carol held a wriggling Maeve on one hip to keep her from making a mad dash for the porch swing.

I stepped back and let them go inside first, pulled the door closed behind us. Any moment I expected my father to turn the corner and stroll down the hallway to greet us, raking back the same lock of thick white hair that always fell into his eyes.

We stepped between two large cardboard boxes, one topped with a pile of smaller boxes and padded mailers. We banged a left toward the kitchen.

"Dad?" Carol said.

We found him hunkered over his laptop at the kitchen table, wearing a crisp white shirt and a blue striped tie over his pajama bottoms.

"Pick me up!" Maeve yelled.

"Grandpa loves you, too, honey," he said without looking up.

I cleared my throat. Our father kept his eyes glued to the computer.

"Hello?" Carol said.

"Time out," our father yelled at his computer. "I've got a wee fire to put out at this end. Back in a flash." He leaned a little closer to his laptop. "Now where in tarnation did they put that thingamabobbie that turns off the camera whoosey?"

Half a dozen senior citizens looked out at us from his computer screen. They were framed in individual boxes that made them look as if they were appearing on a senior laptop version of *The Hollywood Squares.*

Our dad reached for a blob of chewed gum on top of his laptop. He popped it into his mouth for a quick chew, then pressed it over the camera hole.

"Gum!" Maeve yelled.

"Don't you worry, sweetie pie. Gramps won a six-month supply. Sugarless, your mother will be happy to hear."

"What's up with the outfit, Dad?" Carol said.

"No sense putting on pants when the other sweepers can only see your top half."

"Whoa, what is that smell?" I said.

"I beg your pardon." Our father pushed himself up from the chair. Maeve reached her arms out to him and Carol handed her over.

Maeve giggled. She buried her face in her grandfather's neck. "Poophole!"

He kissed her on top of the head. "That's right, your pop-pop loves you. You're the apple of my eye, pumpkin pie."

I sniffed again, followed the smell to the sink. Bowls of half-eaten cereal floated in milk that looked like it was halfway to turning into cottage cheese.

Carol turned on the water. I flicked the switch for the garbage disposal. She dumped and rinsed, while I loaded the dishwasher with one hand and held my nose with the other.

"Nothing like a shipshape kitchen, is there now," our father said when we finished. He handed Maeve back to Carol. "If you girls are finished tidying up, I'll be getting back to work now. We've sniffed out a whopper of a prize and pledged all for one and one for all. It's a snazzy kitchen makeover and whoever wins is going to invite the rest of the sweepers over to Sunday dinner."

Carol pulled a box of cotton candy-speckled cereal from an open carton. "Great. If you win, you can serve them your cereal stash so you don't get diabetes all by yourself."

"Don't you two worry your pretty little heads about the menu. I'm in the running for free groceries for a year. Twenty-five hundred smackeroos, I kid you not."

I opened a box filled with what looked like hundreds of individual packets of salad dressing. "What are you going to *do* with all this stuff, Dad?"

"That's nothing," he said. "One of the fellows won a life-sized cardboard cutout of that Bitsy Spears, although he says she can be good company at the dinner table."

"Britney," Carol said.

Our dad reached over, pretended to catch Maeve's nose between his knuckles. "I need to be getting back to the gang now. Stop by again soon, girls."

. . . . .

"I don't think those sweepers he's hanging around with are a good influence on him," Carol said as I pulled the front door closed behind us. "It's like he's turning into a sweepstakes addict. He couldn't wait to get rid of us so he could get another hit."

"I know," I said. "You don't think it's possible to overdose on breakfast cereal, do you?"

Maeve slid out of Carol's arms and made a beeline for the old metal swing. It was big enough to hold three adults, or as many kids as could pile on, and it had hung from the beadboard-covered porch ceiling from four long metal chains for as long as I could remember.

If I were in charge of the world, every house would have a porch and every porch would have a swing. Sadly, both my own house and John's condo were porch-less, but maybe our next place, the one we'd buy together some magical day in the future when we finally got our collective act together, would have one. And we'd hang a swing just like this.

"I hate to say it," I said. "But even Sugar Butt's starting to look good to me."

"Sugar Butt!" Maeve said. She kicked her feet and giggled as she tried to wiggle her way up and onto on the swing. "Shooo-gah Buttttt!"

"See," I said. "I knew poophole was just a phase. Anyway, we don't even know if this Sally is still in the picture, or even how big an influence she is. And not to defend her, but Dad was already entering sweepstakes before he met her."

Carol gave Maeve a boost. "If we move fast, maybe we can pick the next girlfriend. Preferably someone who knits and likes to take long walks on the beach. After all that time on the computer, Dad could use some exercise."

"And let's not forget the casseroles." I waited until Carol stepped out of the way, then gave Maeve a big push.

A white vintage Mercedes sedan pulled into the driveway. Its tires dug into the lawn as it circled around Carol's minivan and stopped inches short of the garage. All four car doors opened and bevy of blondish women of indeterminate age piled out and made a beeline for the kitchen door. One of them might have been Sally. Actually, any of them might have been Sally.

"No wonder he likes this sweepstakes thing," I said.

Another car, this one domestic and pea green, pulled in. It circumvented Carol's minivan and stopped right next to the Mercedes. Three women and one man got out and followed the first group to the kitchen door.

"Dad's got to love those odds," Carol said. "Do you think we should go in and introduce ourselves, you know, just to be a presence?"

I gave Maeve another push. "I don't think they'd even notice us. But next time we should definitely leave the dirty dishes for them."

Nine

I sat in a kiddie chair at one of the low rectangular tables in my classroom, as I flipped through the résumés and waited for the first candidate to show up. What I really wanted to do was rule them all out simply because Kate Stone had chosen them. Then I'd bring in a ringer myself, someone so perfect for the job that even my bitch of a boss would think I was brilliant to have found her.

I'd emailed everyone I could think of to see if anybody knew anybody who was looking for a low-paying job with basically no benefits. Unless the chance to work closely with me counted as a benefit, which I had to admit was probably a stretch. Sadly, I hadn't come up with a single prospect.

"Hi," June said softly as she passed her former classroom on the way to her new one.

I pretended not to hear her. Then I briefly considered ripping up the classroom circle she'd made on her way out. Maybe I could time all three of the job candidates with a stopwatch as they tried to tape down a new circle, and hire the one who did the best job. In the end I decided to keep June's circle just in case none of the candidates had any more circle-making aptitude than I did.

On the plus side, the first candidate was on time. On the minus side, she looked young enough to be one of the students.

Once Interviewee Number One was seated across from me at the table, I took a peek to make sure her feet touched the ground. She was wearing thin leather flip-flops and a lightweight cardigan over a summery dress. The spaghetti-like ties of a bathing suit top peeked out from under her shoulder-length hair.

"So," I said. "You have a B.A. in New Media with a concentration in Blogging. Do you have any experience working with children?"

"I don't know. Is it on my résumé?" She put her elbows on the table and leaned forward, trying to upside-down read the paper I was holding.

I glanced down at her résumé, as if it might be my job to look it up for her, looked up again. "Do you have any kind of familiarity at all with young children? You know, beyond that you used to be one?" *Like about ten minutes ago,* I was too polite to add.

She stared at me blankly.

"Younger sisters or brothers?" I prompted. "Babysitting?"

She slid her chair back at an angle so she had room to cross her legs. "I have a question. If any of them pukes, who has to clean it up?"

I heard laughter and caught a dual flash of blond hair as June and Ethan walked by my open door together.

I took a moment to regroup. "Why do you think you'd make a good teaching assistant?"

She nibbled the cuticle on her pinky. "It's part time, right?"

"Are you answering my question by telling me you have a particular proficiency at part time work, or are you changing the subject?"

"Huh?"

Her cellphone rang. I looked out the window to give her a moment to turn it off. The poor kid. I was probably completely intimidating her.

"Hey," she said into her phone. "Yeah, I'm still at the first one. The tide's coming in, seriously? How warm is the water? I don't know, hopefully not much longer or I'll be late for the next one. Plus my stomach is starting to growl. Awesome. Yeah, meet me in the parking lot. Mocha Frappuchino. Grande. Yeah, whipped cream. Wait, no whipped cream. Oh, whatever, you decide."

As soon as she hung up, I stood and reached down to shake her hand. "Thanks for coming in, Kristi. You can find your way out."

She stood up, her cellphone still clutched in her hand. "I can?"

. . . . .

I headed for the teachers' room to grab a cup of coffee before the next interview. Not that it made me dislike her any less, but at least Kate Stone had finally sprung for a Keurig. There is nothing like finally getting a quick break in a busy preschool morning and having to settle for a cup of lukewarm coffee sludge because you don't have time to wait for a new pot to brew.

A lazy Susan carousel displayed an assortment of coffee in cute little K-cups. I spun it around a few times and finally settled on a dark roast, organic, free trade special edition. It sounded more exotic than it actually tasted, but at least I made it back to my classroom with time to spare.

I'd thought about waiting and offering a cup of coffee to the second candidate, but if she ended up getting the job, it might set a bad precedent. I mean, who needs a teaching assistant that expects *you* to get her coffee? And it's not like the first candidate had asked me if I wanted her friend to pick me up anything at Starbucks. Which, come to think of it, might have turned the whole interview around.

While I waited for Interviewee Number Two to show up, I sipped my coffee and started cutting letters out of soft purple sponges. I'd bought out the purple sponge stock at all the dollar stores within driving distance to get enough for two complete sets of all twenty-six letters of the alphabet. One set would go out on a shelf at the start of the school year. I'd keep the other letters as back up for when one of the more orally fixated kids invariably chewed the tail off the *Q* or the *P.*

I placed a well-worn oak tag letter *A* stencil on a sponge and traced around it with a purple fine point marker that was just a shade darker than the sponge. I cut out the *A* and placed it in front of me on the table so I wouldn't forget what letter I was on.

There are an infinite number of uses for sponge letters in a preschool classroom. Students can roll out a yoga mat on the floor and use them to pretend to write a story. They can sit at a table and trace the letters on a big piece of paper, or dip the letters in bright colors and sponge paint. Or the whole class can sit around our classroom circle, then I can hand out the letters in alphabetical order, and one by one the kids can hold them up to make an alphabet wave as if we were in the stands at a ball game. We can even do a group rendition of the alphabet song, with each student singing the letter they're holding.

And one magic day, all this play would turn into ac-tual spelling. "I spelled C-O-W," an excited preschooler would proclaim from somewhere in the room. And I'd remember why I loved my job.

By the time I finished cutting out the *D,* Interviewee Number Two was seven minutes late, not a good sign. As Kate Stone had said to me on the rare occasion or two when she'd caught me jogging across the parking lot precariously close to the start of a school day, "It's helpful, Sarah, when the teachers arrive *before* the students."

I cut out the letter *E*, drained the last of my coffee, pushed myself up from my miniature chair. I wandered out to the hallway to get a view of the parking lot. Summer camp was finished for the year and the teachers weren't officially back to work yet, so only a few scattered cars dotted the lot.

A woman my age was standing on the passenger side of a small gray car, waving both arms madly as if she were a traffic controller.

"Great," I said out loud.

I didn't see any way around it, so I pushed open the nearest door.

"Holy rescue, Batman," the woman yelled once I was within earshot. "You have no idea how long I've been standing out here."

I walked around to her side of the car and stopped a safe distance away. " Can I ask you *why* you're standing out here?"

She pointed behind her. She was wearing a long skirt with a bit of a bohemian flair to it. Or maybe the flair was caused by the fact that a big hunk of her skirt was shut in the car door.

"Can't you just open the door?" I asked. Problem-solving abilities were key in a good teaching assistant, assuming this was indeed Interviewee Number Two.

"Now why didn't I think of that? Listen, if you wouldn't mind grabbing my keys—I think they're right under that Jeep—I'd really appreciate it. I'm seriously late for a job interview."

I kept an eye on her as I reached under the adjacent Jeep with one hand and rummaged around until I found a large white key ring shaped like a question mark.

I held it out to her, keeping my distance.

"Okay, this is weird, but would you mind going around and opening the driver's side with the key and then reaching over and opening this door from the inside?"

I took a step back. "Why?"

I was pretty sure I'd read about a scam like this, or maybe I'd seen it on one of those scary TV shows I tried not to watch. The perpetrator sets up a trap by pretending to need help. And then a kindhearted person like me happens by and walks right into it. As soon as I leaned into this woman's car, a big scary accomplice would appear out of nowhere, and I'd be toast.

She gave me a pleading look. "Something's messed up with my car and now the lock clicker thing doesn't work. And the driver's door will only open from the outside. And this door will only open from the inside."

If this was a scam, it could use some refinement. I wish I'd thought to bring my teacher scissors outside with me. That way I could just cut off the part of her skirt that was stuck in the door. And if I couldn't get her to go for that, at least I'd have a weapon.

"It just happened yesterday," she said as I walked around the car. "I haven't had time to get it fixed yet."

I unlocked the driver's side door, looked over both shoulders to make sure nobody was sneaking up on me. I leaned into her car and opened the passenger door. I got back out fast, just in case.

"Thank you so much," she said as I walked back around to her side of the car again. She gave her skirt a shake, adjusted the waistband, fluffed her hair quickly.

I reached out to hand her the key ring just as she was shutting the car door.

A blood-curdling scream filled the air.

Ten

"Are you sure you're okay?" I asked. "Maybe we should reschedule the interview for after the swelling has gone down." *Or maybe cancel it altogether* was what I was really thinking. Even Interviewee Number One was starting to look good to me.

"No, that's okay, I think the ice is helping. And besides, next time I could break a leg. Geesh, I cannot *believe* I managed to slam my finger in the car door."

I glanced down at her résumé. She shifted in her kiddie chair.

"So," I said. "Polly . . ."

"The truth is that my car doors have been messed up for at least a month. Okay, three months. Tops, four. And I should probably warn you that I'm a bit of a train wreck right now."

I looked up. "Ya think?"

"Hey," she said. "I resemble that remark."

"Okay, let's do this. Exactly why would someone with your job history want to become a preschool teaching assistant?"

"How much time have you got?"

I looked up at my classroom clock. "About twelve minutes. At which point Interviewee Number Three will arrive."

"Gulp. Okay, I was in middle management at an increasingly soul-crushing job which ate up the last decade and a half of my life. And then the man I was married to, who talked me into not having a baby because he didn't think it was fair to the kids he'd already had with his first wife, left me for someone else."

"Ouch," I said.

"Yeah. Remember that old T-shirt? The one with the comic book drawing of a woman and a speech bubble that says *Oh my God, I forgot to have children!* Well, that's pretty much me. So, instead of laying off a new bunch of people, which was part of my soul-crushing job, I talked my boss into letting me take one of the layoffs myself so I could get out of Dodge. I grew up a couple towns away from here, so I moved back and found a tiny winter rental right on the beach. I'm sure I'll be wearing a hat and mittens inside to stay warm and there'll be waves in the toilet bowl once the first storm hits, but it was dirt cheap and I've got it until June fifteenth."

"But why *this* job?"

"Two reasons. First, I want more play in my life. I want to sing, play dress up, read fun books that are mostly pictures."

I shook my head. "I hate to break it to you, but our student slots are all filled for the year."

She gave her forehead a quick massage with her good hand. "I get that it's not just about the fun stuff. I have to tell you, if my finger wasn't throbbing so much, I'd be all over helping you cut out those purple letters. I'm a hard worker. I get along with people and I take direction well. I have an iron stomach so I'll never wuss out on you when it comes to mopping up kid messes. I admit that I'm a tiny bit accident prone right now, but I fully believe it's only temporary."

"What's the second reason?"

Interviewee Number Two sighed, shifted in her chair again. Dark circles underscored her amber eyes, and strands of silver ran through her brown hair like tinsel. A sprinkling of freckles danced across both cheeks and congregated on her nose. Even though it was elevated and wrapped in an ice pack, her index finger was well on its way to becoming a breakfast sausage.

I glanced up at the clock again.

"Okay," she said. "The truth is that I'm trying to figure out whether I want to have a kid. You know, by myself. I mean, obviously, I realize I'd need to work out the sperm details. Or maybe I'd decide to adopt. But I haven't spent much time around small children, and it seems to me that's the logical first step, for my own sake, but especially for the sake of a potential child. I mean, it might turn out to be a fantasy that doesn't hold up, you know?"

Interviewee Number Three appeared in the doorway, stepped away a respectful distance.

I looked at Polly. I liked her. I could even imagine hanging out with her. But when it came to hiring her, there were so many red flags flying around her that she could open up her own car dealership.

"Listen, I'm not saying you're going to get this job," I whispered, "but if you do, do not, I repeat *do not*, tell that last part to anyone."

She nodded.

"And please tell me you didn't say anything about it to my boss when she interviewed you yesterday."

"Are you *kidding* me?" she whispered. She leaned over the table. "And by the way, your boss is a total bitch."

. . . . .

Interviewee Number Three turned out to be the perfect candidate. Nicely but not flashily dressed. Sensible shoes. No high maintenance manicure to mess up. Even her hair was pulled back in a practical ponytail.

Her eye contact was good and her handshake firm. She claimed the kiddie chair across from me with quiet confidence, folded her hands together, rested them on the table. Her posture was excellent without being obnoxious.

I moved her résumé to the top of the pile. "Thanks for coming in, Ann. So, let's cut to the chase. Why do you want this job?"

"I've been a stay at home mom, and my youngest is in school for the full day this year. My original plan was to get on the substitute lists at all the Marshbury schools and also take a class or two toward my teacher certification. Give myself a year to start gradually easing back into things. But then I decided to send my résumé to the local preschools, just in case there was a last-minute opening. The hours are perfect and I think I'd be good at it."

She reached across the table and moved the purple sponge *B* down a fraction of an inch until it was lined up perfectly with the *A* and the *C*.

She saw me watching her. "Sorry."

"No, that's good," I said. "Straightening things up is a huge part of the job. Okay, so what happens if one of your kids gets sick?"

"If my husband can work remote that day, he will. My mother-in-law lives in town, so she's the backup. And there are a couple of homeschooling parents in the neighborhood I can call, as long as whatever it is isn't contagious." She paused. "But I'm a mom first, so I can't promise you I won't call in sick if I have to. You do have a substitute list, right?"

"Of course. But it can be a pain in the butt to use it because most of our subs are parents."

She narrowed her gaze a fraction of an inch.

I launched into full backpedal mode. "I meant parents of Bayberry students. The vast majority of them are terrific, of course, but my experience has been that a few, you know, just a really teensy minority—"

"Want to tell you how to do your job, or use their behind-the-scenes access to try to get something extra for their own kid?"

"Exactly," I said. "Wow, you're good."

"There are a lot of people in the world," Interviewee Number Three said, "who have entirely too much time on their hands. My goal is not to turn into one of them."

. . . . .

My boss looked at me across the vast expanse of her redwood desk.

I fought to maintain eye contact, instead of looking away as if I'd done something wrong to end up in her office. Which was exactly how I was feeling.

She gave her Magic Eight Ball a little shake. "*Outlook good,*" she read.

"*As I see it, yes,*" I said, answering her Magic Eight Ball message with my own. Kate Stone relied heavily and painfully on props to create visual metaphors for her meetings. She'd wiggle her wind chimes and tell you to chime in any time. She'd pick up an antique crystal and say the choice was crystal clear. Or open a carved wooden box and tell you to step out of the box. She'd been on her Magic Eight Ball kick for a while now, and it was no more and no less agonizing than the rest of them.

Just in case it might give me some meeting leverage, I'd done my fair share of Wikipedia research. I knew the Magic Eight Ball had a total of twenty messages. Ten of the messages are some variety of yes, five are some type of no, and the remaining five are some version of ask again later.

Since the Magic Eight Ball leaned heavily toward positive messages, it seemed to me that theoretically the odds for this meeting going well should have been better than they actually felt.

There was a lot at stake here. The wrong assistant can be lethal to classroom harmony. Say, an assistant who is always running off to Starbucks or even to the beach. Or an assistant who is constantly losing her keys and has a tendency to slam car doors on body parts, or worse, decides to go hunting for a sperm donor among the Bayberry pool of available or even unavailable fathers. Or an assistant who calls in sick every time one of her own kids doesn't feel like going to school.

Choosing a teaching assistant was a gamble. Kind of like a nonromantic version of *The Dating Game*. Even though the candidates weren't hiding behind a screen onstage while I asked my questions, it's not like a quick interview allows you to truly see someone. How did I really know whether to choose Interviewee Number One, Interviewee Number Two, or Interviewee Number Three? Was it better to think things through logically or go with my gut?

I had to admit my gut didn't exactly have a stellar track record. I'd listened to my gut when I married my former husband. I'd listened to my gut when I hired my former assistant. And they'd both turned out to be traitors.

Kate Stone gave her Magic Eight Ball another shake. "*It is certain,*" she read.

"*Without a doubt,*" I said gamely, even though I was really thinking *Reply hazy try again.*

She shook again. "*As I see it, yes.*" She cleared her throat. "Clearly, Sarah, one candidate is heads and shoulders above the rest and simply our only logical choice."

"*Most likely,*" I said.

I looked over at the Magic Eight Ball, hoping for direction.

Cannot predict now, the Magic Eight Ball messaged me telepathically from the other side of the desk.

Me either, I messaged back. It wasn't really one of the answers, but I thought it sounded like one. Maybe I should take a sabbatical year and get a job updating the Magic Eight Ball responses. I could even come up with a special teachers' edition for stupid meetings like this one. *Yes, your boss sucks, but hang in, the kids are worth it. You have more ability in your little finger than the person sitting across from you has in her entire swelled head. Even though it feels like you'll never make it, you will most definitely live through the year.* I'd probably have to edit my answers a bit to make them shorter. Or maybe the manufacturer could just make the teachers' edition Magic Eight Ball bigger to accommodate them.

Concentrate and ask again, the Magic Eight Ball signaled.

Instead, I shifted in my chair and waited for my bitch of a boss to put her cards on the table first. I was pretty sure I was going to give logic a try this time around. Logically, Candidate Number Three was the way to go, since she was the only one who had any firsthand knowledge of actual children, which seemed like a reasonable prerequisite.

Kate Stone placed a piece of paper in front of me on the table. "Shall you call her or shall I, Sarah?"

I looked down at the résumé she'd chosen. I looked up at my stupid boss.

"*My reply is no,*" I said.

Eleven

"I don't get it," my sister Christine said. "Your boss picked the assistant you were planning to pick, right?"

"Poophole!" my niece Sydney said.

"You got that right, honey," I said. "She totally is. And that's why I couldn't go along with her."

"Helpful," Christine said. "First her cousin teaches her the word and now you're reinforcing it. No wonder your boss wanted to choose your next assistant."

"Oh, don't be such an oophole-pay," I said.

"Oophole-pay!" Sydney yelled.

I'd gone right from my powwow with my stupid boss to watching my sister Christine's kids for a few hours. Every year, right around this time, my siblings practically lined up to get as much childcare as they could out of me before I disappeared back into my classroom for another school year. Carol ran her own event planning business. Christine was a freelance digital designer and also worked just enough hours at Old Navy to spend her entire paycheck keeping her family cheaply and trendily dressed on her employee discount. I hated to shop, so the perk for me was that every once in a while she threw a cute pair of jeans or a couple of tank tops my way.

Now Christine, Sydney and I were sitting on the floor in my living room having a tea party with a tea set I'd borrowed from my classroom for the occasion. Sydney's older brother Sean was stretched out on a beach towel under a tree in my front yard reading a book.

I sipped a thimble-size cup of tea and tried to chill.

I'd been almost positive that Candidate Number Three was the way to go. Until I looked down and saw that hers was the résumé Kate Stone had placed in front of me.

No way, my gut screamed.

Even the Magic Eight Ball agreed. *My reply is no*, it messaged me telepathically.

I knew that Candidate Number Three, aka Ann, was the clear logical choice. She was a mom. She knew the ropes. But I couldn't get Polly out of my mind. I'd been a train wreck too when my former husband left me. What if I'd decided to get out of Dodge? And I'd rented a tiny house where I didn't know a soul. And I needed a job, someone to take a chance on me?

Logic jumped out the nearest window.

I looked Kate Stone right in the eyes. "Polly is my choice. She's smart and she has a great attitude."

"She's entirely overqualified, and she has absolutely no experience with children. She won't last the school year."

"I'm the one who has to work with her, and I think she'll be spectacular. And I'm willing to put in the necessary time to train her correctly." I stood up. "I'll call her this afternoon."

Kate Stone gave her Magic Eight Ball one more shake. "*Outlook not so good*," she read, or pretended to read.

"I'll take my chances," I said.

Convincing Kate Stone to let me choose my own assistant had been a big victory for me. But instead of celebrating my success, what I was feeling now was one big nagging doubt: What if my boss was right?

I shook my head to bring myself back to my living room. I followed Christine's glance as she looked out the window to check on Sean.

"It's so great that Sean's turning into a reader," I said. "And I can't believe how big he's getting."

Christine sighed. "I know—so grown up. You were right about his speech, by the way. He's saying most of his words correctly now, but I'm still glad I had him work with a speech therapist over the summer."

Sydney tried to force-feed her doll some tea, then sopped it up with a napkin.

"I kind of miss the way he used to talk," I said. "Remember how cute it was when he was in his car and truck phase and he couldn't say fire truck?"

"Don't." Christine pushed herself to a standing position and scooped up Sydney. "I think it's time to grab your brother and head for home, honey. Say thank you to Auntie Sarah."

Sydney spread her arms wide. "Firefuck," she yelled. "Firefuck, firefuck, firefuck!"

· · · · ·

I dialed Polly's cellphone number.

She picked up on the third ring. "If you call me one more time, I will smash this phone into a million pieces and/or file a restraining order. You're not my husband anymore, Jonah. You're my *was*band. Which means you have to leave me alone. Until. Death. Do. Us. Part."

"Ooh, that's good," I said. "Do you mind if I write it down and file it away in case I ever need it down the road?"

"Who is this? Just so I know whether to hang up or not."

"It's Sarah. Hurlihy? From Bayberry Preschool?"

"Oh, hey. Sorry about that. I don't usually answer my phone without checking to see who's calling, but I can't seem to find my reading glasses."

I didn't say anything.

"Okay, I stepped on them. But they're just nonprescription cheaters, and I ordered a whole case so I'll be good to go as soon as they get here. Priority shipping. I got a great deal, so let me know if you want the website or anything."

I hesitated. It wasn't too late. I could tell Polly I was calling to say that even though she didn't get the job, I hadn't wanted to leave her hanging. And I was sure she'd find the perfect job in no time. And, well, I wanted to wish her all the best in her next chapter.

. . . . .

I switched my phone to the other ear, leaned back against my headboard. "Are you sure you don't mind me not staying at your place tonight? I hate to mess up our schedule."

"Schedules are made to be messed up," John said.

"Thanks. It's not that I don't want to see you. It was just such a long day that I'm not sure I have enough energy left to drive all the way to Boston."

"I get it. And this way I can head in to work early tomorrow. My plan is to try to get enough done that I won't have to work remote even once while we're gone."

"Yeah, I was thinking I'd like to get my classroom pretty much set up before we leave so I don't have it hanging over my head."

"Okay, then. How about we check in tomorrow to see how much progress we've made and plan our next sleepover accordingly. And in the meantime, we'll let a little absence make our hearts grow fonder."

"Mine's already pretty fond."

"Why, thank you, m'am. And ditto."

"Ditto?" I said.

John laughed. "So, which candidate did you end up hiring? Wait, let me guess."

I smiled, switched my cell back to the original ear. I crossed my legs, took a sip from the glass of white wine I soooo deserved after my stressful day.

John took a sip of something on his end. "You hired the train wreck after all."

"She's not a train wreck. Well, maybe a little bit, but she, *Polly*, thinks it's only temporary, and I do, too. How did you know that's who I picked?"

"Because I know you, Sarah. You're kind and generous and you have a big heart. And you and I both know what it's like to be in her shoes."

"Ugh, don't remind me. When I called to tell her she had the job, she thought I was her ex-husband and told him to leave her alone. She called him her *was*band."

"Much nicer than some of the things my ex-wife used to call me. And I'm embarrassed to admit I went on a bit of an obsessive calling streak myself when my ex and I first split up. You know, tell me what you want me to do, who you want me to be. Completely over the line, but at the time I guess I was too far gone to stop myself."

"Actually, Polly said her husband left *her*. For another woman."

"That doesn't mean he doesn't want her back."

I started to tell John the whole story. About how Polly had wanted children, but her wasband talked her out of it because he already had them. And how one of the reasons she wanted to be my assistant was so that she could spend time around kids. Because even though

Polly was my age, give or take, she was thinking about having a child. On her own.

I'd been so sure my own ex and I would have kids. It was encoded in my suburban Boston Irish Catholic DNA, something my family just *did*. But Kevin was never quite ready. And then he was gone, and now rumor had it that he had not one, but two children. I'd never told a soul that I'd dreamed, repeatedly, about Kevin pushing a double stroller away from me on the other side of town while I screamed at him to give me back my babies.

Other than that, I'd pretty much put the kid thing out of my head. My biological clock was probably barely ticking anymore. My life was filled with kids already. Sometimes I still felt like a kid myself.

Part of the reason I didn't tell John this portion of Polly's story was that she'd told it to me in confidence. That kind of sharing between women, even if it was technically oversharing in this particular case, and even if Polly and I weren't exactly friends, was sacred. You didn't just repeat it to the next person, even if he was your significant other and even if you knew he'd never let on that he knew if he ever met the storyteller in person.

But I was pretty sure that the real reason I didn't share the rest of Polly's story with John was that I didn't want to dredge up all those old feelings again. With the passing of time, my disappointment about not having children had gone from devastating to an occasional dull throb. I might not even want them anymore.

And then there was the fact that John's and my relationship was relatively new. We were still figuring things out. What if he thought I was telling him Polly's story in order to gauge how he felt about last-ditch efforts to have children?

And what if he was right?

I pulled myself back to the phone. I scrolled through our conversation, trying to remember the last thing John had said.

"So you really think Polly's wasband might want her back?" I said. "I didn't even think of that. With my luck they'll probably make up over the weekend. And then I'll be back to square one in my assistant search."

"Didn't you say she's already rented a place on the beach for the winter?"

"Good point. Maybe I can talk her into just being pen pals with the wasband until the lease and the school year are up. Or maybe we'll let him visit occasionally on weekends."

"Sounds like a plan. Listen, Horatio is standing by the door with his leash in his mouth."

"What do you think he's trying to say?"

"Ha. Just give me a minute to grab some treats and we can take this conversation for a spin around the block."

"That's okay," I said. "I think I'm going to turn in anyway. You guys have a good walk."

"Okay. Say good night to Sarah, Horatio."

Horatio was still barking his goodbye when I hung up.

I sat there on my bed for a while. Even though it was my choice not to stay at John's condo tonight, now I felt sad and alone. Like everyone in the whole wide world but me was connected to somebody else at this very moment. As if I could write down all their names, scattering them randomly across a poster board, then take out a ruler and draw neat pencil lines matching them all up. My father to his girlfriend du jour. My siblings to their spouses. Polly to her wasband. John to Horatio.

At the end of the day, at the end of it all, sometimes I thought I'd be the only one not paired to someone else, like the cheese that stands alone in "The Farmer in the Dell."

Twelve

Carol, Christine and I were sitting on my sofa, each with a tablet or laptop perched on our lap. Our polish-toed, flip-flop-clad feet were resting on my coffee table. We all even had our ankles crossed the same way, right over left.

Since mine was the only house without kids running around in it, it was our go-to place whenever we needed to get a plan and wanted to hear ourselves think at the same time.

"Maeve did *too* teach Sydney to say poophole," Christine said.

"You have no way of knowing that," Carol said. "Sydney might have taught it to Maeve. Or maybe they both heard somebody say it on *The View*."

"I think the best thing to do is to keep them apart for a while," Christine said.

Carol took a sip of her wine. "You are such a drama queen, Chris."

"Takes one to know one," Christine said.

"Knock it off, you two," I said. I'd gotten up extra early and made a list of all the things I wanted to accomplish before John and I headed off on our road trip. *Lug some more stuff into classroom. Clean out refrigerator. Do laundry. Buy deodorant.* I'd been checking things off the list ever since. I was finally just about ready to call it a day when my sisters showed up. Apparently I'd forgotten to put our previously scheduled dad summit on my list.

"It's a good thing I brought wine," Carol said. "And I can't believe you have basically nothing in your fridge."

I sighed. "That's why God invented takeout. And you both totally owe me for babysitting, so you're the ones who should have thought to bring some food to thank me. Plus, did you see how *clean* my refrigerator is? You can practically see yourself in the produce drawer."

By the time our spinoccoli pizza was delivered, we were almost ready to stop insulting one another and get to work.

Carol took a bite of pizza and put it back down on her paper plate. "Okay, so I was right. Sweepstakes Sally is bad news."

"Oh, puh-lease," Christine said. "How do you know that?"

It drove Christine absolutely crazy that Carol always knew everything before the rest of our family did. As far as I could tell, Carol's position as the family know-it-all was the only thing Christine had ever wanted that she couldn't get.

"I have my ways, little sis." Carol smiled, reached for her wine, took a self-satisfied sip. "Anyway, *Sally* puts out a weekly sweeps newsletter, heavily sponsored by companies who want their own sweepstakes promoted, and backed up by a huge presence on Facebook, Twitter, and Pinterest, which makes her even more appealing to potential sponsors."

"Nothing wrong with Dad having a girlfriend who makes a good living," Christine said. "And you have to admit she's got to be pretty smart to have figured all that out."

Carol ignored her. "But her real money seems to come from reeling in what she calls her Sweeps Dream Team. She charges a monthly membership fee and offers incentives for each member to pull in more members."

"Whoa," I said. "That sounds like some kind of pyramid scheme. Sweepstakes Sally gets richer and richer, and all the poor suckers like Dad win an occasional case of beet juice."

"What kinds of incentives?" Christine asked.

Carol sipped her wine, left us hanging.

"Come on," I finally said. "Tell us."

Carol put her glass down, stretched, recrossed her ankles. "Rumor has it that the big incentive is private one-on-one coaching. Sally makes the senior men think she's hot for them and then they do anything she wants them to do."

"Ohmigod," I said. "Dad has totally taken the bait. Not to mention the hook, the line, and the sinker."

. . . . .

Carol's first idea was to distract our father with another woman.

"I don't think so," I said. "He's too far gone. You should have seen him when he stopped by my house with her. Totally gaga."

Christine let out a puff of air. "He stopped by your house with her? Why didn't he stop by *my* house with her?"

Carol and I gave each other a quick glance. One or both of us might have rolled our eyes.

"It was no big deal," I said. "He just had to drop off something for my classroom."

"What?"

I shrugged. "Sidewalk chalk."

My younger sister shook her head. "Sean and Sydney love sidewalk chalk. Why did *you* have to get it all?"

One thing I've learned is that if you spend your life looking for the things you didn't get, you're always going to find them. The only annoying part was that I could see this behavior in somebody else so much more easily than I could recognize it in myself.

"Fine," I said. "I'll split the sidewalk chalk with you. But you have to give me one of your kids."

"Sure," Christine said. "Which one? Never mind, I can buy my own sidewalk chalk."

Carol cleared her throat. "Are we done with the *Daddy likes you better* nonsense now?"

Nobody said anything.

"Good," Carol said. "Because we all know he likes me the best anyway. Okay, moving on. I still don't think it would hurt to get Dad's personal ad out there again. I checked and it's no longer running in the *Marshbury Mirror*."

The *Marshbury Mirror* was the local weekly. Our father's ad had been running in it pretty much constantly since he'd started dating again about a year or so after our mother died. Since most of its readership had moved on to digital dating by now, the small paper had recently done away with the personals section in the print edition. They were still taking our father's money, but all the ads were clumped together in one section now. The last time I'd seen it, his had been positioned between the chimney sweep and the cat sitter.

"Uh-oh," I said. "If Dad stopped his ad, that definitely proves he's fallen hard. Usually he just pretends he forgot to cancel it when he's dating."

"So," Carol said, "we'll just have to move his ad to a place where Sweepstakes Sally is less likely to stumble across it. And it wouldn't be a bad idea to broaden Dad's dating horizons a bit at the same time. I mean, at this point it's not like there are all that many women left in Marshbury he *hasn't* dated."

"Good point," I said. "What about a senior dating site? I read somewhere that they're really big right now." I didn't mention how encouraged I'd been. It was good to know that if I managed to screw up my own life yet again, at least I might be able to look forward to successfully dating once my AARP card arrived. Or maybe it was my Medicare card I'd have to wait for. Either way, there was a faint glimmer of hope down the road.

"Sounds like a plan." Carol reached for her iPad. "Okay, let's do it."

Christine and I grabbed our laptops.

"One-two-three, Google," Carol said.

With lightning speed, we all pulled up encouragingly long lists of senior dating sites.

"I'll check out Grow Old Along With Me," Carol said. "It has a nice poetic ring to it."

"I hosey Sexy Senior Singles," Christine said. "As long as the pictures don't turn out to be X-rated or anything." *Hosey* was our childhood way of staking a claim, something I didn't realize was unique to New England until I'd gone off to college. If you added *black, white and red on top infinity*, it meant you really, really wanted it.

"Okay," I said. "Then I call dibs on Perfect Rematch. It's optimistic, but not too optimistic. Playful, but with a nice sense of history."

"What are you, a dating site critic now?" Christine said.

"At least I could be," I said. "Unlike some of us who've been married so long they can't even remember dating."

"Focus," Carol said.

Once we'd finished checking out our senior dating sites, we couldn't agree on which one to use. Basically because we all wanted to use the one we'd found.

"Look," I said, "they all offer free trials, so what's the big deal? We can each set up an account for him at a different site. Let's just make sure we all use the same password, so it doesn't get confusing."

"Okay," Carol said. "The password is D-A-T-E."

"Hey," I said. "That was my password."

"So?" Carol said. "You're not using it anymore."

"But it has sentimental value," I said.

"Fine," Carol said. "We'll make it DATEDAD."

"Ooh," Christine said. "We could even tweak his ad a little bit for each site so it's like A/B/C testing."

"Awesome," I said. "Let's make it a contest. The winner gets the first decent date-baked casserole that shows up."

"You two can do what you want," Carol said, "but I'm going to stick to Dad's original ad. It's tried and true."

"Good point," I said. "That ad sure has worked for him."

"How does it go again?" Christine said.

Carol and I began to recite our father's personal ad in perfect sister harmony. After the first few words triggered her memory, Christine joined in.

HONEST, HOPELESSLY ROMANTIC, old-fashioned gentleman seeks lady friend who enjoys elegant dining, dancing and the slow bloom of affection. WM, n/s, young 50s, widower, loves dogs, children and long meandering bicycle rides.

"No way can we leave him in his fifties," Carol said when we finished. "It's been a while since he's seen the young side of seventy."

"And he's not exactly a big dog-lover," I said. "Though I think he's mellowed on that considerably, so maybe we should just leave that part in there."

"We should definitely leave it in," Carol said. "Dog bait is a powerful force in the dating world."

"But I think we have to take out the bicycle part," Christine said. "Bike riding could be dangerous at his age, even with a helmet. Oh, wait, a friend of mine just bought an elliptigo. It's like a cross between an elliptical machine and a scooter—much lower to the ground, so it's not as far to fall."

"Must love long meandering elliptigo rides," Carol said. "It's brilliant. The single senior ladies will be lined up for miles."

Christine rolled her eyes. "You just hate it because I thought of it first."

"Knock it off, you two," I said. "Let's get these ads posted so we can move on."

A rare and lovely silence filled the room as we released our father's profile back into the virtual dating world.

When we'd finished, Christine topped off our wine.

We held up our glasses.

"To Dad," I said. "May all the good ones rise up to meet him. Preferably carrying excellent casseroles."

"May the wind always be at their backs," Carol said. "Blowing all the classy senior ladies in his direction."

"And may Mom continue to keep a close eye on things from heaven," Christine said.

There was a moment of silence as we each thought our own sad thoughts.

"To Mom," Carol said, and we held up our glasses again.

"Sometimes," I said, my voice almost a whisper, "when I wake up I still forget she's gone, just for a second."

"Me, too," Christine said.

"I think it's always going to be like that," Carol said. "For the rest of our lives, no matter how old we get."

I gave one of my eyes a quick wipe.

"All the senior ladies," I sang, repurposing that old Beyoncé song.

"All the senior ladies," Carol and Christine sang.

We stood up, did a little dance around my tiny living room as we sang, wiggling our hips and pretending to put a ring on it.

"We've still got it," Christine said when we finished. "At least I do."

"Maybe we should video it with one of our phones and put it up on YouTube," I said. "We would soooo go viral."

"We sure would," Carol said, "but not necessarily in a good way. Okay, the next part of the plan is that we become sweepers, too. That way we can crash this dream team party and find out what's really going on."

"Holy Nancy Drew," I said. "I love it."

Thirteen

Lorna was getting out of her car when I pulled into the Bayberry Preschool parking lot.

I parked, grabbed a laundry basket overflowing with classroom stuff from my trunk.

Lorna slowed her pace just enough to let me catch up with her.

"What are you doing here?" I said. "You're not turning into one of those teachers who spend half their summers here kissing up, are you?"

She shifted the two huge plastic shopping bags she was carrying so they didn't drag on the ground. "Wait till you see the brilliant idea I came up with. I found all these great floor pillows on clearance at Marshalls, and I'm going to turn one corner of my new classroom into a sushi bar. The kids will sit on floor pillows around a low table. I bought a bunch of packages of those cute little rectangles of seaweed. A batch of rice and some diced cucumbers and shredded carrots, and I'll have my students making their own California rolls to snack on in no time."

"Mmm," I said. "If there's one thing I've learned over the years, it's that preschool kids just can't get enough of the taste of seaweed."

Lorna didn't say anything.

"And remember, if the kids sit on the floor, you're going to have to sit down there, too. Maybe it's just my knees, but I think it would feel like a long way down by about the third week of school or so."

"So what. It's *authenticity*, Sarah. Cultural authenticity."

"Just tell me you didn't cut off the table legs yet."

Lorna dropped both bags to the ground. "The saw's still in the car."

"See, you're fine. You'll mix up some flour-and-water paste, and the kids can make seaweed collages. The floor pillows will be perfect for your reading nook."

Lorna kicked one of her plastic bags. "Every preschool classroom in the universe has a reading nook."

"Imagine that," I said. "I wonder why."

Lorna kicked the other bag.

"Listen," I said. "You're an incredible teacher. You don't need sushi snacks. You don't need sawed-off table legs. You just have to keep being your phenomenal self."

Lorna picked up her bags. "Follow me."

. . . . .

Lorna and I dropped off our stuff in the hallway outside my classroom.

I followed her next door to her former classroom. She gave a quick knock, waited, looked over her shoulder.

She turned the doorknob.

"This is so rude," I said. "How would you like it if—"

"*Shh*." She pushed the door open a crack and disappeared inside.

She was my friend so I followed her.

Lorna's former classroom looked like it had morphed into the set of a Disney movie. Three-dimensional flowers climbed one wall and reached for a sparkly painted sun smiling down from the ceiling. Styrofoam clouds circled the sun like big puffy pillows. On the far side of the room, black chalkboard paint sliced through the length of two walls and a snippet of ceiling, transforming day to night. Randomly placed stick-on stars actually glowed against the dark paint. The Big Dipper hung from the ceiling. Next to it, a hanging cow jumped over a hanging moon.

"Holy show off," I said.

Tucked into the nighttime corner was a reading nook partitioned off by a sturdy plywood divider that looked exactly like an open book. The book cover side was painted in green chalkboard paint. Two white horizontal lines painted on the cover waited for the students to fill in the title with chalk and add their own names as the author.

I walked around to check out the other side of the partition. Artfully arranged floating shelves, already stocked with an assortment of picture books from *Where the Wild Things Are* and *Don't Let the Pigeon Drive the Bus* to *Llama Llama Red Pajama*, graced the inside of the giant book. Brightly colored floor pillows tucked into the cozy little corner created by the open book made me want to curl up, put my thumb in my mouth, learn to read all over again.

"Wow," I said, "I hate to give it to him, but this is really cool."

And then I saw it. Tucked into another corner, right next to the door to the storage room where my former assistant would be most likely to disappear.

A meditation chair. It was made out of wood and sat low to the ground, wide enough to sit on cross-legged. A thick sage-colored cushion covered the seat, and a lotus blossom was carved on the base. A laminated circle of poster board, a necklace of yarn strung through it to turn it into a pass, was already hanging from a little hook on the adjacent wall at the perfect preschool height. *Chill out*, it said.

A good teacher knows how to take a liability—in this case June falling into deep meditation at the drop of a hat—and turn it into an opportunity so the kids could learn a new life skill. How had I missed it?

"I picked up that chair in Bali years ago," Ethan's voice said behind us. "It was only collecting dust in my storage unit, so I figured it might as well get some good use."

I froze.

Beside me, Lorna yanked out an earring.

Since she was one who got me into this, I let her turn around first.

"Hi there," she said. "Fancy meeting you here."

I forced myself to face him. "Hey," I said. "Nice decorating job."

"Actually, we were hoping you'd be here," Lorna said. She held out the earring on the palm of her hand. "Hey, you didn't happen to find an earring that looks like this, did you? I think I might have lost it in here, you know, before the enforced classroom redistricting took place."

"Thanks," Ethan said in my direction.

He turned to Lorna and smiled his toothy white smile. He pointed. "You might want to check your other ear."

. . . . .

Lorna and I didn't say a word until Ethan's door was safely closed behind us.

"Wow," I said.

"It's well beyond *wow*," Lorna said. "It's even beyond *holy crap*."

We stopped outside my classroom door.

Lorna picked up her big plastic bags. "Face it, we're doomed. As soon as the kids get a look at that room, their parents are going to be lined up outside the principal's door trying to get them switched to Mr. Buchanan's class."

I crossed my arms over my chest. "So. Let them go. More work for him, fewer students for us."

"You and I both know it's not going to play out that way. What's going to happen is that Kate Stone will kick into overdrive. Classroom inspections. Extra staff meetings. Even though he's still completely wet behind his ears, she'll probably even make Lover Boy head up some kind of classroom decorating committee."

"I think you're overreacting."

"I'm *not* overreacting. Our only hope is that one of his students impales himself on the back of that ridiculous chair on the first day of school."

"That's the spirit." I reached for my laundry basket. "Come on, Lorna, let's just dump our stuff in our classrooms and go take a nice long walk on the beach while we still can."

Lorna shook her head. "I've already put in an emergency call to my assistant. And I suggest you do the same. Oh, wait, did you hire a new one yet?"

"Yeah, I did. It was a tough call, but her name is Polly. I think she's going to be great. Either that or—"

"Call her." Lorna said as she walked away.

"Thanks for listening," I yelled after her.

I opened the door to my classroom and dropped the laundry basket on the floor. Then I headed for the teachers' room to make a cup of coffee.

. . . . .

Polly was spinning the K-cup carousel, squinting at the coffee assortment.

"Hey," I said.

She jumped. The carousel tipped over. An army of little white coffee pods rained over the edge of the counter and rolled across the floor.

"Oh, boy," my new assistant said. She squatted down, started picking them up.

I joined her.

"Would it be stating the obvious to mention how embarrassed I am?" she said.

I reached for a runaway K-cup. "Relax. It could have happened to anyone. Well, maybe not anyone, but at least you don't need ice this time around, which is definitely a step in the right direction."

"Thanks." Polly dropped a handful on the counter and went back to chasing little coffee pods.

"What are you doing here anyway?" I asked.

"I had to come in and sign my paperwork. The office manager was giving me a tour when a phone call came in that she had to take. So she told me to wander around and get comfortable. I was just trying to decide whether helping myself to a cup of coffee would be getting too comfortable."

I stood up, blew any potential dust off the K-cups I was holding, started pushing them into the empty circles in the carousel. "How about we both grab some coffee and go drink it in your new classroom? Unless there's someplace else you have to be?"

"Nope. I'm pretty much free for the rest of my life." She lifted the lever that opened the top of the Keurig with her good hand. She held up the used K-cup that was in it. "What happens to these?"

I pointed to the wastebasket. A crowd of foil-topped white plastic pods rested on a pile of crumpled institutional brown paper towels.

Polly cleared her throat. "I was just wondering— what if we emptied them and then cleaned them out. Maybe the kids could use them for some kind of lacing activity?"

I looked at her.

Polly blushed. "If it's a stupid idea, just tell me straight out. I can take it."

Fourteen

Who knew that a coffee pod is not quite as easy to clean out as you'd think it would be. First, Polly and I had to peel off the foil, working slowly to get all of it because the edge of the foil was glued to the top of the circular plastic rim. Next, we had to shake the used coffee grounds into the wastebasket and then rinse the little plastic cup under the classroom faucet. Only to find that the K-cup was completely lined with a tiny coffee filter that was glued all the way around, just under the rim.

"Eww," Polly said. "This is kind of making me second-guess all that glue you and I are drinking along with our coffee."

"Get over it," I said. "We're going to need a lot more of these little suckers. I've got some other ideas for them, too."

Polly held a K-cup between her thumb and middle finger, her still swollen index finger pointing skyward. She poked a hole in the filter with the index fingernail of her good hand and managed to pull out most of it. She scraped unsuccessfully at the glued part of the filter, then held out the K-cup for me to see.

I was already filling the sink with warm water. "I think we're going to have to soak them first and then scrape off the rest with a knife."

Once the coffee pods were clean, dry and good to go, Polly carried them over to one of the tables, while I grabbed a handful of plastic-tipped shoelaces and a few other things from the supply closet.

"First of all," I said. "Your lacing idea is brilliant. So much more interesting than yet another cardboard lacing card."

"Thanks. My first idea was to use wine corks."

If I'd just taken a sip of my coffee, I would have spit it out. "Ha. That would really fly in a preschool. We'd have all the kids going home and asking mommy and daddy to drink up so they can have the cork for their teachers."

"Yeah, I had a feeling."

"Plus, how would we make the holes for the laces?"

"I was thinking we'd use a corkscrew. You know, sideways."

"Hmm," I said. "That just might have worked. And to continue the theme, we could have covered one whole wall in here with corks and turned it into a bulletin board."

"And made a cork wreath for our door. We could have changed it out seasonally."

"Ooh," I said. "We could have carved one end of some corks into shapes to make little stamps—you know, the kids would dip them in paint and then press them onto a sheet of paper. And we could even have put a whole bunch of corks in a plastic bucket for a cork-counting activity."

Polly grinned. "I think I've done that at parties. Oh, and maybe we could have started a wine blog on the side. Just to diversify."

I reached for a K-cup. "Which would have been a good thing. Since we'd both be out of a job within a week."

"Don't worry, I'll be sure to check my pockets for corks before I leave my house on workdays." Polly grabbed a shoelace. "So the kids will push one end of the shoelace through this little hole in the bottom that the coffee comes out of, and then pull the lace out the top?"

I'd already thought this part through. "I don't think so. The hole is way too small and close to the edge. Plus preschoolers' fingers are usually pretty short, so some of them won't be able to reach far enough inside the cup to grab the shoelace tip." I reached for a package of dot stickers. "So I think what we'll do is cover the bottom hole with one of these. Then we'll use this paper punch to make two holes across from each other and halfway down the sides of the K-cup."

I did a trial run, ran a shoelace through the new holes, held it up.

Polly grabbed her own coffee pod, covered the bottom with a bright red dot sticker, punched two perfectly executed holes in the sides. When she finished, she threaded a shoelace through both holes. Then she tied a knot in the shoelace and hung it over her head like a necklace.

"This is awesome," she said. "You could even carry a snack around in it."

"Feel free to wear one home. And grab a handful of Cheerios from the closet to fill it up."

"Don't tempt me." Polly smiled, picked up another empty cup, reached for the paper punch. "Listen, Sarah. I just want to thank you again for taking a chance on me. I can't even tell you how much this job means right now."

"You're welcome," I said. "I think we'll make a great team. But I have to tell you, we're going to need to come up with something a little flashier than coffee pods to start the year off." I described Ethan's classroom decor in complete covetous detail.

"Wow," Polly said when I'd finished. "I'd love to see it. Do you think it would be okay if I introduced myself to him and asked for a tour? Especially since we're both, you know, new and everything?"

I thought, just for a moment or two, about giving her a heads up. But about what? That Ethan might be sleeping with our bitch of a boss? And/or my former assistant? It seemed ridiculous now. Saying it would only make me appear less than professional, even gossipy. Besides, Polly was old enough to have been around the block a few times. She could take care of herself.

"Go right ahead." I pointed. "His room is the next door over that way. Do me one favor though, okay?"

Polly stood up, untucked her hair from behind her ears, gave it a quick fluff. "Sure, what?"

"Let's just keep your coffee pod idea to ourselves for a little while. Things can sometimes get a little bit competitive around here, so it's good to have an ace or two up our sleeves."

She gave me a thumbs-up with her good hand. "Got it."

As soon as Polly left, I lost myself in K-cups. I broke out the poster paint and painted two pods each red, blue, yellow and green to make a color matching activity.

I added three dried beans to each of two pods, half-filled two more pods with sand, and dropped little jingle bells into two more pods. Then I covered the tops with circles of duct tape. Presto—the students would be able to shake the pods and match up the sounds.

I spooned some pumpkin pie spice into two pods, some baby powder into two more, and stuffed half a cotton ball soaked in lemon extract into two more. Then I covered the tops of the pods with identical scraps of thin fabric, which I held in place with tightly circled rubber bands. Abracadabra—a smell matching activity.

I was almost out of K-cups when true inspiration struck. Preschoolers love to play Go Fish, but holding their cards spread out—so that they can see them all but the other players can't—can be a big challenge for their stubby little fingers.

I turned a K-cup over so the open side faced down. I made a quick slice through the bottom and halfway down the sides with a safety razor to create a slot for the cards. I broke out our deck of Go Fish and arranged five cards into a fan-like hand. I tucked them into the slot and let go. The cards didn't even wobble.

Polly and I could slide the cards into the slot for each Go Fish player and they'd be all set to play. We could also use the slotted pods as sign holders. Or personalized place markers at the table. Oh, the possibilities were endless.

I was so in the zone that I lost track of time until I ran out of coffee pods. My first thought was to drink more coffee. I checked the classroom clock, realized that if I had another cup at this hour of the afternoon, I'd never sleep tonight.

I tried to remember how long Polly had been gone. A half hour? An hour? More?

I briefly considered going next door to check up on her. But seeing Ethan again so soon after being caught trespassing in his classroom wasn't exactly appealing. Maybe I'd just hang around a little longer and get some more work done until Polly showed up again. But if I waited for her, I should probably offer to take her on a quick insiders' tour of Marshbury, maybe buy her a celebratory ice cream cone. I hadn't even asked her how things were going in her new rental, her new town, her new life.

I stopped myself. Becoming new best friends with your assistant was never a good idea. It could make for a long school year, especially if your assistant forgot that a big part of her job was to let you boss her around.

I put my supplies away, wiped down the table, and left a note for her on the table.

Polly—

Great working with you today. I'm heading off on a quick vacation, but enjoy your last days of freedom and keep those cork-free ideas coming. See you soon!

—Sarah

. . . . .

I was just pulling into my driveway when my phone rang. Lorna.

"Just for the record," I said as soon as I pushed the green button. "That's the last time I follow you anywhere. Getting caught in the new teacher's classroom was ridiculously embarrassing."

"Oh, get over it. Listen, does your assistant have medium longish dark hair with a little bit of gray in it? And freckles? Pretty but not obnoxiously so? Our age, give or take—you know, at her zenith?"

"At her zenith?"

"Her peak, her apex, her highpoint. Like us."

I decided it wasn't worth pointing out that Lorna was more than ten years older than me. Then I considered whether or not I should buy into the idea that I was not only still at my zenith, but that I had at least another decade of zenith-hood to look forward to.

"Well, does it? Does that sound like your assistant?"

"Could be," I said, "especially if she was wearing a black jean skirt and a white T-shirt. And holding a swollen finger up in the air. Why?"

"Bingo."

"Bingo?" I repeated.

"Guess who just climbed into a big white truck with Lover Boy and drove off?"

I took a moment to consider whether or not it was possible to lose not one but two assistants to Ethan before the school year even started.

"I'm sure it doesn't mean a thing, Lorna," I said.

"Mark my words," she said. "This guy is trouble."

Fifteen

"Pretty please, Dad?" Christine said. "With sugar on top?"

"Yeah, come on, Dad," I said. "You know what they say—the family that sweeps together keeps together."

Carol didn't bother to say anything. She just sat down at the kitchen table and fired up her iPad. Christine and I put our laptops down on the table, following our big sister's lead like we usually did. We all claimed the same chairs that had been ours when we lived here.

Our dad sighed, reached for the wad of gum perched on his laptop, covered the camera hole so that the individually boxed-in seniors looking out from his screen couldn't see us.

He pushed his wayward clump of white hair out of his eyes. "Listen, kiddos, God knows I love ya to the moon and back, but the other sweepers might think you're crampin' their style. They're not as easygoing as I am when it comes to sharing their turf. Truth be told, some of them can get pretty darn nasty."

Carol leaned over so she could see his screen. "Dad, you do realize they can still hear you, right?"

"Are you sure about that?" Our dad tilted his head and leaned closer to his laptop. "Testing one, two, three. Now where in tarnation did they put the thingamahoosie that keeps things private around here?"

Carol tapped his mousepad a few times to turn off the sound. "You're all set, Dad. You can say anything you want about your friends now."

He leaned back in his chair and crossed his arms over his chest. The pajama bottoms he wore beneath his dress shirt today were covered with tiny blue sailboats that matched the stripes on his tie. "Okay, let's make this snappy so I can get back to work. What do you want to know?"

"Everything," Carol said. "We're beyond fascinated."

Our dad's eyes looked skyward. He shook his head, imploring the heavens to give him strength. "Que Sera Sera," he began to sing in his best Doris Day imitation, though he actually sounded more like Frank Sinatra. The rest of us joined in for a little impromptu family sing-along. Our harmony could use a little bit of work, but it didn't bother us one bit.

We gave ourselves a round of applause when we finished. Our dad put two fingers in his mouth and let out his famous whistle. My sisters and I did our best to imitate him, something we'd been doing with more or less success since childhood.

"All righty now, enough with the monkey business," our father said as if he hadn't been the one to start it. "How about if one of you girls opens a thingamahoosie or three over there and rustles us up some grub while I give you the run down? Your poor old dad's been working so hard to bring home the bacon he can't remember the last time he strapped on the feedbag."

I weighed the possibility of having to cook against finding some good stuff for my classroom. My classroom won out. I skipped over the padded envelopes and went right for the boxes. The first one I opened contained spray-on moisturizer, each tall-necked aluminum can safely contained in its own little cardboard compartment. I pulled out a few cans and walked them over to the table.

My sisters each grabbed one.

"Hey, get your own," I said.

The second box I opened was filled with men's knee-high trouser socks. I dropped a few pairs on the table in front of my father. "Don't forget about these, Dad. They'll look pretty snazzy with your pajama bottoms."

I was just about to let one of my sisters take the next shift when a plethora of assorted pasta peered up at me from a new box I opened.

"Score," I said. "We'll be swimming in pasta necklaces for months."

"If it's all the same to you, Carol," my father said, "I prefer mine with a little bit of sauce on it."

"And if it's all the same to you, I prefer my father to call me by my real name," I said. "Which, by the way, happens to be Sarah."

The real Carol got up, filled our old dented spaghetti pot with water, turned on the stove. Christine joined me in the search for something to accompany the pasta.

Christine opened a box and held up a granola bar.

"Too crunchy," I said.

I pulled a bag of pork rinds from another box.

"Eww," Christine said.

"Hey," our father said. "Don't knock it till you've tried it. Now be a good girl and hand that bag over here lickety split."

Christine and I finally unearthed a case of assorted pasta sauces. We ruled out the more pedestrian ones and decided to go for the black truffle alfredo sauce.

Our dad looked up from watching his soundless sweeper buddies on his computer screen. "You girls have what you want, but I like my spaghetti sauce red if you don't mind."

"Come on, Dad," Carol said. "Live a little."

"Yeah," Christine said. "I hear black truffles are incredible with pork rinds."

Eventually we decided to warm up two different sauces to keep everybody happy. Once the meal was underway, we joined our father at the table.

"So, Dad," Carol said, just like we'd rehearsed it. "What do you think about this one?" She slid over with her iPad so he could see the screen.

Upgrade Your Dad Sweepstakes
His home is his castle, so give your dad a majestic man cave to call his own, including a 72-inch flat screen TV, a luxurious faux leather recliner with dual beverage holders, his own fully stocked minibar, and much more from the Upgrade Your Dad Sweepstakes. Enter to win once daily per person/email.

"Whoa, baby," our father said, just like we knew he would.

Christine opened her eyes wide, blinked a few times. "So, Dad, is this something you might like your favorite daughters to try to win for you?"

"You're darn tootin' I would. I can see that 72-incher up over the fireplace mantel already. I'll even let you kids watch it with me. But the chair's mine."

"Well," I said, "we sure can't think of a dad who deserves to win this more. So as soon as you show us how to enter, we'll be all over it. And maybe you should take us to one of your sweeper meetings just to make sure we're doing everything correctly." I sighed, laid it on thick. "I've been a little bit lonely lately, so I think it would be good for me to get out and meet some people. And I could use a new hobby."

"Not on your life," our dad said. "We're keeping this one under our hats. Those other sweepers can come over and visit once in a while, but that man cave is all mine and we're not taking any chances with it."

He wiggled his fingers like a piano player warming up for a performance. "Okay, kiddos, now synchronize your computers and let the master show you how it's done."

By the time the pasta was on the table, we were all officially entered in the Upgrade Your Dad Sweepstakes. Not just with our regular email addresses but with about eight new ones each.

"Now any time you get an extra minute," our Dad said, "you just make up a new email thingamabobbie and enter again. Keep a running list and make sure you hit them all once a day like clockwork."

I twirled some pasta around my fork. "Just curious, but is this legal?"

"Of course it's on the up and up. It makes the companies running the sweepstakes look good to be swimming in entries. I wouldn't have told you about it if it was any kind of funny business. Your mother would never let me get away with it."

Our father took a slug of beet juice. "Now don't forget to call your brothers and get them in on the action. And your friends, too, as long as you can trust 'em not to try to get their mitts on my man cave. You've got to watch some of these people like a hawk. It's the Wild West out there all over again."

We never even heard a knock. Sally just appeared in the kitchen doorway, the frazzled ends of her blond hair touching the shoulders of what looked like a designer jacket, at least to my discount store eyes. I followed her tight-legged jeans down to her red shoes with their kick-butt pointy toes and nosebleed-high heels.

Our father smiled up at her. "Pasta?" he said.

"Billy," she said, "we've got a Sweeps Dream Team meeting in twelve minutes on the other side of town."

She took in the table full of computers. "What's going on here?"

"Just helping my girls out with some homework, sweetheart," our father said breezily, even though it had been decades since his girls had needed homework help.

He patted his mouth with his napkin. He gave Sally his most dazzling smile as he pushed himself up from the table. "What's cookin', good lookin'?"

She tapped a manicured fingernail on the face of her gold watch.

"Now hold your horses, hon. Just let me kiss my kiddos goodbye and I'll be right with you." He strolled around the little kitchen table, giving us each a peck on top of the head. Then he held his elbow out to Sally, who looped her arm through his and started propelling him toward the door.

"Dad," I said. "Don't you think you might want to put on some pants first?"

"Shoes wouldn't hurt," Carol said.

Sally sighed.

"Back in a flash," our dad said. He grabbed a pair of socks from the table. "You wait right here and catch up with the kiddos, sweet pea."

We listened to the old stairs creak as he made his way up to the bedroom.

The three of us looked at Sweepstakes Sally. She looked down at her phone. Her thumbs danced.

"Sally," I said. "I don't think you've met my sisters yet. Carol, Christine, meet Sally. Sally, meet Carol and Christine."

Sally looked up, nodded, didn't quite make eye contact.

"Nice to meet you," Carol said. "And I'd like to make it abundantly clear that we consider ourselves to be personally responsible for our father's well-being."

"Nice to meet you," Christine said. "And, just so you know, we're watching you."

"Very carefully," I added.

Sixteen

John and I were wrapped in each other's arms, post-sex smiles spread across our faces.

"Well, that was fun," I said.

"It certainly was," he said.

I reached down and yanked the top sheet over us again. John's sheets were so much nicer than mine. His pillows were, too. If we ever actually made it all the way to moving in together, clearly my bedding would be relegated to backup.

John reached under the sheet and traced a circle around my jeweled navel with one finger. My pierced navel was a souvenir from a brief walk on the wild side I'd taken while chaperoning my niece Siobhan on a piercing expedition. It had been a while now since Siobhan's and my adventure, and I had to admit I was pretty much over the whole pierced belly button thing. The truth was that it had a tendency to rub against my clothing and had ultimately turned out to be more irritating that liberating. But the diamond-studded navel ring John had surprised me with was the first present he'd ever given me. Maybe I could have it made into a belt buckle.

I traced a circle around John's unpierced navel. Wondered if we could just stay here, marooned on his bed, wrapped up in the satisfying thread count of his linens, for the rest of our lives. Things were simpler here. Clearer. It was only when we got out of bed that everything got complicated. What was our next step? Who would give up what to make it happen?

John propped himself up on his elbows, nuzzled my neck, leaned in for a long kiss.

"Have I told you lately that I love you?" he said when we came up for air again.

"Ditto," I said.

He laughed.

Horatio whined from the other side of the door.

I sighed.

John was already sitting up in bed. "Well, you have to admit he was pretty patient this time. Why don't you stay right there, and I'll take him for a quick walk around the block before we turn in for the night."

I rolled over to the edge of the bed, reached for my clothes. "That's okay. I have to get up anyway. I forgot to enter to win a sweepstakes for my father. He'll kill me if I don't enter at least eight times today."

John put both arms through the sleeves and swung his T-shirt over his head. Men and women really were from different planets—not in a million years would I put on a T-shirt like that. "Your family is endlessly fascinating, I'll give them that."

I put my head through the neck of my own T-shirt first, then rooted around for the armholes. "Easy for you to say. You don't have to be related to them." John's own parents were happily ensconced in an active adult community halfway across the country. He had a much older sister he hardly ever talked to. So far he actually seemed to like my big, boisterous, invasive family, at least in small doses.

I stood back while John opened the door. Horatio went crazy, as if he'd been separated from John for decades. John squatted and scratched Horatio's chest. Horatio jumped up, put his paws on John's shoulders, covered his face with kisses.

I gave them a moment. Then I reached down and scratched Horatio behind one ear. He didn't exactly jump up and down in excitement, but he didn't try to chew my hand off either. We'd come a long way, John's dog and I.

John grabbed the leash while I scooped a handful of treats from the treat jar. This was our ritual now, and I knew that my being the go-to treat person when I was around was a big part of the reason Horatio put up with me.

The three of us walked along John's well-lit, well-groomed, condo-lined urban street. John held the leash with one hand, his other arm draped over my shoulder,

Horatio stopping to lift a leg at every vertical surface we passed. I tilted my head back so I could see the thin swathe of stars not blocked by tall buildings twinkling down at us.

"If we were at my house, we could be walking the beach now," I said.

"If we were at your house, I'd already be thinking about the ridiculous commute ahead of me tomorrow morning."

We walked quietly for a while, our silence broken only by the soft ripple of plastic when John unfurled a poop bag from the roll attached to Horatio's leash. On the one hand, I appreciated that John was the kind of guy who would always clean up after his dog, even under the cover of darkness. On the other hand, for the rest of our walk, the arm that had been around my shoulder was now extended out to John's side, a lumpy little bag dangling from his hand.

John poured Horatio a fresh bowl of water when we got back to his condo and then grabbed two bottles of water from the fridge for us.

I sat on a barstool at his granite-topped kitchen island and entered the Upgrade Your Dad sweepstakes for my father, over and over again.

John sighed a long dreamy sigh. "Do you believe we only have two more nights until we leave?"

I laughed. "Two more sleeps, my brothers and sisters and I used to say."

"We used to have a calendar hanging in the kitchen, and my sister would lift me up so I could cross off the days until it was time for vacation."

"Just promise me you're not going to have to say *are we there yet* every five minutes for the whole ride."

"Scout's honor," he said.

I groaned. "You're not going to try to start a campfire by rubbing two sticks together or anything, are you?"

"Don't think I'm not up to the challenge."

. . . . .

Instead of waking up to the warmth of John's body next to mine, he was already in the shower. I briefly considered joining him there. Instead I slipped into an old terrycloth bathrobe of his that I commandeered when I stayed over and stumbled to the kitchen in search of caffeine.

Coffee was sputtering from his stainless steel coffeemaker. Horatio had clearly been walked and fed, since he wasn't dancing around with his leash in his mouth. He was curled up on the low modern sectional calmly chewing on a stuffed squirrel.

I poured a cup of coffee, sat on a barstool, stared into nothingness until John emerged.

"Hey," he said. His hair was lightly jelled and his contacts were in place. He was dressed for work already.

"Hey yourself," I said. "Back in a flash."

He stopped me for a kiss. I angled my morning breath mouth away so the kiss landed on my cheek.

I turned on the fancy brushed chrome faucet at one of John's his and her granite-topped master bathroom sinks and brushed my teeth. Then I pinned up my hair with an old banana clip I kept in my purse and climbed into John's enormous walk-in shower. I did a quick cleanup, then sat for a moment on the wide travertine-tile bench and watched the water pour down on my feet from above like a spring downpour. John's master bathroom was a gazillion times bigger and more luxurious than the one and only bathroom in my little three-bedroom '70s ranch.

An egg, bacon, and cheddar sandwich on a toasted English muffin was waiting for me on a clear glass plate when I got back to the kitchen. This I could get used to.

I took a big bite. "Mmm, delish. Did you make it from scratch?"

John laughed.

"They do come frozen, you know. But this is way better." I took another quick bite, then wrapped a napkin around my breakfast. My shoulder bag was already slung over my shoulder. "I'll eat the rest of it on the road so we can get going."

"Are you sure?"

"Of course. Sadly, I eat most of my meals that way."

John turned off the coffee maker, slid his laptop into a leather briefcase. "So what's the plan? Are you going to come into the office with me so you can visit with the Gamiacs? I just have to drop off Horatio at puppy play care first—it'll only take a minute."

"Maybe next time. I still have a lot I'd like to get done before we take off on our road trip, so why don't you just drop me off at the T." The Boston subway system was called the MBTA, but everybody always shortened it to the T.

Unfortunately, there was nothing short about the trip ahead of me. The T would eventually take me to the commuter rail station, where I'd jump on a train that was more luxurious and even had Wi-Fi. If the stars were aligned, I'd be back at my trusty old Civic, which I'd left overnight at the Marshbury train station, in under two hours.

Driving was quicker, especially if you were going against the commuter traffic, as I would be this morning, but also infinitely more aggravating. John's condo had a garage, but each unit had only one designated parking space, and finding curbside parking could easily eat up the time I saved by driving.

John pulled me in for a hug and a quick kiss. He smelled like sandalwood soap and Mitchum deodorant. I'd borrowed both, so I probably did, too.

"Thanks for doing the heavy lifting on this visit," he said as he locked the door behind us.

"Fair's fair," I said. "But, boyohboy, do I wish I could wiggle my nose like Samantha on *Bewitched*— Elizabeth Montgomery, not Nicole Kidman—and suddenly be home. Are you sure you don't mind me skipping the office visit?"

We took the staircase down to the parking garage, so we didn't have to wait for the elevator.

"Not at all," John said. "I should roll up my sleeves and get right to work anyhow. I've got a one-on-one with my boss at ten. And I was thinking I'd take a longish lunch and do some shopping—pick up some new toys for Horatio to keep him busy in the car on the drive to camp. And maybe a new collar so he'll look dazzling in case he hits it off with a new lady friend there. He's got an appointment with the groomer today at puppy play care—they bring in a groomer once a week. Makes it convenient."

"Great," I said. "Maybe I should make an appointment with a groomer before we take off, too."

He laughed. "You look perfectly groomed to me already."

"Thanks." I pulled out the ancient plastic banana clip I'd just remembered and gave my hair a shake. "So what's the plan for tomorrow morning? Do you want to stay over at my place tonight and start this road trip of ours from there?"

John clicked the car doors open. "By the time I pick up Horatio again and get us both packed, I guess the traffic should have died down a bit. But we'll both be beat by then. So maybe it makes more sense to leave at the crack of dawn tomorrow. How about I pick you up at five?"

"A.M.?"

"It's either that or get stuck in traffic."

"But you'll have to drive all the way to Marshbury, then turn around and go back in the same direction."

"It's not that big a deal. We'll just take Route 128 and jump on the Mass Pike. And before we know it we'll be at Camp Winnabone."

From the backseat, Horatio barked in excitement.

John reached back and gave him a quick pat. "I'm with you, buddy. The three of us are going to have one tail-wagging good time."

Seventeen

I spaced out the whole way home, not really thinking, not really not thinking either. It was like I was in limbo, lost between two worlds, just floating.

Growing up, the nuns at Saint Stephen's, the elementary school my siblings and I had all attended, told us that the little babies who died before they were baptized were banished to a place called Limbo—always capitalized—where they would float around for the rest of eternity. Also sent to Limbo were the people who had died without having sinned quite enough to go all the way to Hell, but who needed to work off some un-confessed smaller venial sins before St. Peter would open up the pearly gates and let them into Heaven. But at least the trivial sinners had a chance of getting out of Limbo someday. The babies didn't have a prayer.

I used to toss and turn while I tried to sleep, worrying about all those poor little Limbo babies. I pictured them no bigger than my thumb, stretched out on individual cotton balls floating in the air, surrounded by swirls of fog and puffs of clouds, a locked gate that led to Heaven hovering above them. Did the poor little babies have to lay around in their birthday suits, or did they wear diapers? And if so, who changed them? Who fed them? Who sang them to sleep at night? And how could this heartbreaking place have the same name as the dance we did under a pole at birthday parties, and why did you have to capitalize one and not the other?

Like Limbo was something I'd needed to worry about when I was in my formative years. No wonder I couldn't get my act together. I was probably still traumatized.

It wasn't that I thought of John's place as Hell, or even hell. It was a beautiful condo in a beautiful city. John thrived there—it was the perfect fit for him. But even if I could imagine living at John's place, which I had to admit I couldn't, I definitely couldn't picture commuting to my job at Bayberry from there.

I knew lots of couples survived far longer distances—even cross-country commutes—for years. So, on the one hand, I had a lot of nerve whining about John's and my totally doable trek. But on the other hand, you can do anything as long as you have an end in sight. For John and me, I couldn't see an end in sight.

I was sure there were some great preschools in John's neck of the urban woods—they might even pay better than Bayberry. But I didn't want to teach at another school. For all its imperfections, I loved my classroom and I loved my job. I had friends there. I could roll out of bed and be at work in less than five minutes. If I forgot something, I could go get it and be back before anybody missed me.

My students had plenty of room to play outside. Soft grass to roll around on, their own playground. My assistant and I didn't have to walk them to the nearest city park, the kids holding on tight to a long rope stretched between us so we didn't lose anybody along the way.

But it was more than that. I could breathe in Marshbury. The houses weren't built on top of one another. I could see the sky. Every once in a while mine would be the only car on the road. I could walk the beach anytime I wanted to. Sure, there was only one tiny movie theater in town, one grocery store. And the sidewalks pretty much rolled up by 10 P.M., even earlier on weeknights. Although, to be fair, there were five package—aka liquor—stores.

People who lived in the city always talked about how much more there was to do there. Theater and museums and restaurants and concerts. But how often did they really take advantage of these things? And it's not like you couldn't drive in to the city for them. Once in a while, that was no big thing—it was the everyday commute that I couldn't imagine surviving.

I leaned back in the half-empty commuter train and stretched my arms out to the sides. I had the double seat all to myself on this leg of the trip, the perk of commuting in the wrong direction.

Maybe what was really going on here was that John and I were stuck in that old Aesop's fable about the town mouse and the city mouse. How had that story ended anyway? I was pretty sure I had the book some-where, either at home or at school.

. . . . .

I was finally home, sitting in my office. I'd scoured my bookshelf and the books I'd boxed up for my class-room and managed to find Jan Brett's *Town Mouse, Country Mouse* as well as a Little Golden Book version of *The Country Mouse and the City Mouse*, both based on the fable.

I could totally relate to the country mouse, sitting here as I was in my suburban ranchburger. I hardly ever even had any food in my fridge. When John visit-ed, he probably took a page from the book and thought, *My poor girlfriend! I do believe an ant could eat better!*

John's city mouse life was richer, a splendid feast of granite countertops and restaurants that offered take-out well into the night. I flipped through both versions of the fable to refresh my memory about exactly how it all went down. Just as the two mice were settling down to their abundant city feast, a big scary cat crashed their party.

So yay, or *yea* as they said back in Aesop's fable days, the moral of the story was that a simple life filled with peace and quiet and walks on the beach is better than a richer one filled with danger and conflict. I knew it.

I was the town and country mouse. John was the city mouse. But who was the cat? Maybe Horatio used to be the cat, but by now the two of us had worked things out so he was no longer a threat. So maybe the cat was the vulnerability I felt when I was out of my own element. Or maybe I just needed to get a cat. After all, John had a dog, so fair was fair.

I closed both books, which I had to admit weren't really helping as much as I'd hoped they would. My phone rang. Carol.

"Sorry," I said by way of answering. "But there's no way I can babysit for you today. John and I are taking off on a road trip first thing in the morning, and I've got a zillion things to do between now and then."

"Siobhan is watching the younger kids for me. Christine is dropping off her kids at a friend's house."

"Great," I said. "Thanks for the update. Let's catch up again real soon."

"Wait, wait, wait," Carol said before I could hang up. "Sweepstakes Sally found out about the personal ad we placed for Dad, and she freaked out. Christine and I are on the way over now to talk him down from the ledge. Meet us in the driveway. Now."

"Why is it," I said, even though Carol had already hung up on me so I was technically talking only to myself, "that there's always some kind of family drama whenever I'm trying to get packed for a trip? Or accomplish anything else, for that matter."

Since there didn't seem to be an immediate answer to that particular existential question, I hung up my own phone. I transferred some dirty dishes from the sink to the dishwasher, put on an old pair of yoga pants and a raggedy T-shirt, threw all my camp-worthy clothes into the washing machine.

I grabbed my purse and keys from the tiny entryway table.

"This better be good," I said out loud.

. . . . .

Our father was sitting at the kitchen table, his white hair sticking out all over the place. He wasn't even half-dressed for work—he was wearing a plaid pajama shirt and matching pajama pants.

"She's kicked me to the curb, my Sal," he said. "She thinks I'm some kind of two-timing philanthroper. I told her I'm true blue through and through, but she's not having any part of it."

"What happened?" I said, hoping he thought he'd screwed things up with Sally on his own, which meant my sisters and I weren't going to be in trouble.

"She thinks I'm stepping out on her."

"Imagine that," Carol said. The thing about our father was that his blarney level was so high that even when he was dating behind one of his girlfriends' backs, he simply thought of it as double dating.

"Take a gander." He pointed to his laptop screen. Our father's ad peered up at us from the Sexy Senior Singles site.

"Gee," Christine said. "I wonder how that got there."

Our dad pounded his fist on the table. "I know exactly how it got there. They were having a slow day on the internut, so they did one of those searchamacallit thingamabobbies and the rest is history. You can't blame a fellow for being a legend in his own time, can you now?"

"Dad," Carol said. "I think the more important question is: If the two of you are a couple, what was Sally doing on Sexy Senior Singles?"

"Wow," I said. My sister Carol could drive me crazy, but I had to admit she was good. "Yeah, Dad. You deserve a girlfriend who's fully committed, not someone who's looking over her shoulder for somebody better."

"Exactly," Christine said. "Takes one to know one, by the way."

A heavy silence pulled up a chair and joined us at the kitchen table.

"What did you just say?" I finally said.

"Nothing," Christine said.

I glared at her. "Are you insinuating that I'm looking over my shoulder for somebody better?"

Christine got up, started opening boxes.

I followed her. "Are you implying that *John* is?"

"Keep it down to a dull roar over there," our father said. "Some of us are trying to ruminate over here."

It had been quite a few years since I'd pulled one of my sisters' hair, but I was close. "Tell me what you meant, Christine."

She opened another box, started pulling out bottles of hand sanitizer. "I'm just saying you haven't fully committed, that's all."

"Mind your own beeswax," I said. "You have no idea what you're talking about, *by the way*."

"Hello-*oh*," Carol said. "Today's catastrophe has already been scheduled. We're trying to help Dad find a new girlfriend, remember?"

"Bite your tongue," our father said. "Our Sally is the only gal for me. All's we have to do is get her back."

"Look, Dad," Carol said as she slid her iPad over to him. "What a surprise. Your ad made it up on the Grow Old Along with Me site, too. And it looks like fifty-two women have answered it already. I know it's hard for you to let Sally go, but don't worry, everything's going to be just fine."

Christine and I were already firing up our laptops. I pulled up the Perfect Rematch account I'd set up for him, started scrolling through the seventy-three responses.

"Ooh, Dad, check out this one," I said. "She even looks a little bit like Sally."

Our father sighed, leaned back in his chair, closed his eyes. "Not interested. I only want the real Sally. I had a romantic trip all planned for the two of us. Ernie, he's one of the sweepers, won one of those trailers shaped like a canned ham a ways back. He's even got a truck with one of those hitcheroo jobs on the back to pull it wherever you want it to go. He said I could borrow the whole shebang for as long as I needed it. I was just about to spring the surprise on Sally when my ad hit the fan."

"Her loss," I said. "Dad, I know it's hard, but I think you've just got to move on. Remember when you told me Kevin wasn't on his best day good enough for me? Well, we didn't want to hurt your feelings, but the truth is we think you can do a lot better than Sally."

Our father put his hands over his ears.

Carol slid his laptop over so she could use it. She typed away for a while. "Okay, ready to go now, Dad. You're logged into all three dating sites. You don't have to date any of these women until you're ready, but I think it's only polite to reach out to a few of them just to say hello so you don't leave them hanging."

"Exactly," Christine said. "It'll probably make their day just to hear from you."

Our dad uncovered his ears. "You girls run along now. You don't think you could cook up another quick batch of that spaghetti before you go, do you? Your old dad needs to keep up his strength."

Christine cooked while Carol and I took turns trying to get our father to open his eyes. "Look, Dad," Carol said. "Henrietta wants to meet you. See how pretty she is? It says she loves to cook and take long walks in nature. She's a nurse—"

"Ooh, Dad," I said. "You know how you love nurses. Maybe she wears one of those cute white dresses with the zipper . . . white stockings . . . a perky white cap . . ."

"You don't have to get all kinky, Sarah," Carol whispered.

"Sorry," I whispered back. "I was just trying to get a little bit of a mood going."

Our father kept his eyes closed.

"Ooh," I said. "How about this one, Dad. Her name is Jasmine and she's a certified massage therapist. Just saying."

"Barb loves poetry," Carol read. "You could practice your Browning on her."

"Poppy has a spot open on her co-ed bowling team," I said. "They have team shirts and everything."

Eighteen

Eventually Christine finished cooking the pasta and warming up a jar of sauce. She put a heaping plate on the table in front of our father.

"Dig in, Dad," she said in her cheeriest voice.

"Mmm-mmm," Carol said. "That sure does smell good. Come on, Dad, eat."

Our father kept his eyes closed, but we could tell he was hanging on by a thread.

I got up from the table and opened a cabinet, chose two avocado green Tupperware containers that had to be at least thirty years old, split the leftovers between them. I popped one into the fridge and carried the other one back to my place at the table.

Carol and Christine looked at me.

"What?" I said. "It's dinner. No sense duplicating efforts."

"See," Carol said. "You can't even commit to food."

"Back off," I said. "I mean it. And if you two have been talking about me behind my back, you'd better knock it off right now."

"Fine," Christine said. "But don't come crying to us when you screw up your life again."

Since my father's eyes were closed, I gave my sisters the finger.

"Okay, I'm out of here." I stood up, grabbed my laptop and my Tupperware container.

I put my hands on my father's shoulders, patted his messy hair down a bit, kissed him on top of the head. "I'll catch up with you later, Dad. John and I are leaving on a road trip in the morning, but I'll have my cell with me if you need me. And I think Poppy's message is the one you should answer first. You know how they say nothing soothes the soul like bowling."

"Yeah, I'm out of here, too," Carol and Christine said at the exact same time.

"Owe me a Coke," they both said.

I tried to stomp off ahead of them, but they stuck to me like preschool paste. The thing about sisters is that they think they have the absolute right to insult you and then act like nothing happened.

"He's fine," Carol said as the three of us clomped across the front porch. "His eyes might have been closed, but he was definitely listening. He'll have a new girlfriend in no time. Our work here is done."

. . . . .

I drove straight to the beach. The parking lot was beginning to empty out, so I found a space right away. Couples and families and solo beach-goers carried beach chairs and umbrellas and coolers and wagons filled with sand toys along the boardwalk to their cars, like a pilgrimage in reverse.

By this time in the late afternoon, the sun had out-maneuvered repeated applications of even the highest SPF sunscreen, and noses and shoulders were getting pinker by the minute. Coarse Marshbury sand had worked its way under damp bathing suits. More sand hung on anywhere it could get a grip. Even if you had an outdoor shower at home, some of this sand would find its way into your house, and you'd remember the beach every time you crunched across your scratched wooden floor.

I put my car into Park, lowered the windows, breathed in the sharp salt air. A sea breeze cut through the heat, a hint of cooler fall air twirling just below the hair-frizzing humidity.

I looked down at the ancient plastic container occupying my passenger seat and contemplated what shape my meal would be in if I let it swelter in a closed car while I walked the beach. I had to admit that 4 P.M. was on the early side for dinner, but if I ate it while it was still lukewarm I wouldn't have to microwave it later.

I opened my glove compartment in search of an eating utensil. I struck pay dirt—a plastic knife, fork, spoon and napkin all wrapped up in a plastic takeout pouch.

"Meant to be," I said.

As I ate my solitary meal, I watched the parade of people through my windshield as if I were at a drive-in movie. Toddlers screamed, teenagers texted, a Boomer couple paused for a kiss. Everybody appeared to know exactly where they were going. They each seemed to have a destination. An actual plan for their lives.

I tried to twirl some spaghetti around my inadequate plastic fork. Gave up, shoveled some in the direction of my mouth, sucked in a long, slurpy strand. Growing up, my brother Michael had called it *pissghetti,* and even though the rest of us could pronounce the word correctly, we'd all switched over because it was so much more fun to say that way, almost as satisfying as a swear word.

A ridiculously good-looking couple approached as if they'd stepped off the cover of a magazine. They looked so put together they probably didn't even have sand in their bathing suits. As they passed my car, they both gave me and my dinner a quick glance, then looked away.

"Take a picture," I said. "It lasts longer."

I finished eating, delicately licked my fork clean, patted most of my mouth with the flimsy paper napkin. Then I put the top back on the Tupperware container so my car didn't reek of tomato sauce when I got back to it.

I clicked the doors locked and strolled up the boardwalk, stepping off onto the sand to let a family and all their paraphernalia pass, then stepping back on again. At the end of the boardwalk, I kicked off my flip-flops, squatted down, looped two fingers through the thongs to carry them. Which reminded me that we used to call them thongs instead of flip-flops when we were kids, back in the days before the word thong relocated to the domain of underwear.

The tide was low and getting lower. I stepped over clumps of sundried seaweed and assorted debris at the high tide line, leaving my footprints in the damp hard-packed sand on my way to the water. I splashed in the warmish, at least by New England standards, late summer ocean, then hung a right and walked along the foamy water's edge, occasionally stepping over a jellyfish or a ruffle of wet seaweed.

It used to be that at low tide you could walk the length of three Marshbury beaches, one connecting to the next one and then the next. But coastal erosion had changed all that, its unrelenting ferocity taking out the beach houses in its path. At high tide, ocean met seawall in some areas these days, completely erasing the beach for hours at a time.

Even now with most of the tide out, it was a much shorter walk than it had been just a few years ago. More beach was slipping away every year. Just like my life.

"Whoa, Sarah," I said. "Hea-*vy*."

A seagull squawked overhead.

"I know, I know," I said, "But it's true."

A couple walking in the other direction didn't even give me a second glance when they passed. The good thing about talking out loud to yourself these days is that instead of thinking you're crazy, people just assume you have Bluetooth and you're on the phone.

When the beach gave way to big barnacle-covered rocks, I turned around. I swung my arms, picked up my pace, watched a sailboat crisscross the horizon.

Why did I have to overthink this? I loved John. He loved me. His dog tolerated me. I'd made some extra money this summer consulting for the company John worked for, so I didn't even have to worry about paying my bills for a while.

I didn't have to micromanage my life. Instead, I just had to go with the flow and trust that things would find a way of working out down the line. I'd stay in the moment, enjoy my road trip with John. Since the whole camp thing clearly meant so much to him, I'd even rustle up my happy camper smile.

I squatted down to pick up a perfectly heart-shaped beach pebble. The first time I'd found a heart-shaped rock as a little girl, I'd asked my mother if the ocean did this on purpose.

I turned it over in my hand, still wondering.

Nineteen

When John's headlights lit up my driveway, I stumbled out of my house with my suitcase and locked the door.

John popped his trunk open, gave me a kiss, tucked my suitcase in next to his. Then he let Horatio out for a quick pee on my front lawn.

Horatio jumped back in the car. John opened the front passenger door for me, shut it again once I'd managed to crawl inside.

"Coffee," I croaked. "Wait, what time does Dunkin' Donuts open?"

John smiled, turned on the interior light, reached for a backpack at my feet and pulled out a stainless steel thermos. He took off the cover that doubled as a cup, unscrewed the top carefully. A swirl of coffee-scented steam rose as he poured.

"Thanks," I said. "I might just live through this road trip after all."

He held up the backpack. "Granola bars," he said. "In three flavors. Plus individual packets of almonds, sunflower seeds, and trail mix. Help yourself."

From the backseat, Horatio let out a funny little sound, part snore, part yelp.

John turned to check on him. "Asleep again already," he reported. "And probably dreaming about camp. I think he's almost as excited as we are."

"Mmm," I said. "I bet."

We headed for the highway, the dark Marshbury streets dotted with the occasional glow of a streetlight. Almost nobody else was insane enough to be on the road this early, so we made it to the highway in record time. I fought to stay conscious while I sipped coffee and waited for the caffeine to kick in.

"How about a little music to keep us awake," John said.

"Sure." I reached for the radio.

"It's in the backpack," John said. "I couldn't find all the songs I wanted to download to make us a playlist, so I had to order a CD."

If I'd been more awake I might have seen it coming, but finding *101 Best Camp Songs* was a total surprise.

"You don't think it's too early for this?" I said.

"Of course not. It'll get us in the mood."

I couldn't think of an alternative, so I slid the CD into the slot and pushed Play.

John jumped right in and started singing along to "Hello Mudda, Hello Fadda."

I groaned softly into the thermos cup.

"Come on," he said once the song mercifully ended. "Join me. As a preschool teacher, I thought you'd be all over this."

"As a preschool teacher, I have to save my voice for my classroom. It might even be in my contract that I'm not allowed to sing during road trips."

John jumped right into "The Ants Go Marching." Then he sang along to "Dem Bones Gonna Rise Again" and "Goober Peas" and "Flea, Fly." He had a nice voice, but that didn't make me want to jump out of his car any less.

I gritted my teeth. Dawn was breaking in stripes of pink and blue as we pulled up to the entrance to the Mass Pike. The machine spit out a toll card, and John grabbed it without missing the sneeze in "On Top of Spaghetti."

"Are we there yet?" I said.

"Down By the Bay" finally wore me down. I sang along with John about the bears in their underwear and the snakes with their bellyaches, and when we got to the woo-woo part, we both screeched it out.

"See," John said, "I knew you'd get into it."

"Shhh," I said. I launched into the first verse of "Boom Boom Ain't It Great to Be Crazy" without missing a beat.

We sang "Do Your Ears Hang Low" and "Barges" and "A Bear Went Over the Mountain" and "Found a

Peanut." Once we'd finished the last stirring notes of "Kumbaya," John reached over to pause the CD.

He put on his blinker, switched lanes. "Do you know that this song was first sung in a creole language called Gullah by people living on the coastal islands of South Carolina? They were actually saying 'Come by here, my Lord,' though the word *kumbaya* has since come to mean the relentless optimism you feel when you become part of a warm cohesive community like camp."

"Fascinating," I said. "I must have missed that feeling. All I remember from Girl Scout camp is that the entire point seemed to be to try to find a way to sneak over to the Boy Scout camp across the lake."

John's History of Kumbaya lecture over, he cranked up the camp tunes once again. We sang and sang, and I even picked up a couple of new old songs for my classroom. In this era of crazy overreaction, you had to be careful though. Take "Kookaburra," for instance. One flavor of crazy parent might worry about the possibility of that *gay your life must be* line sending preschoolers toddling down the path to homosexuality. And how about that wonky messaging in "A Boy and a Girl in a Little Canoe?" A parent at the other end of the crazy spectrum might insist that we change the lyrics to make it clear that the girl doesn't have to kiss the boy in the little canoe unless she *wants* to.

We stopped at the next rest area so all three of us could take a bathroom break. Then we walked along a little path through the woods to stretch our assorted legs. If I blocked out the sound of the 18-wheelers whizzing by on the highway, I could almost pretend we were at camp already. It wasn't half bad.

Branches of tall pines stretched to greet one another over our heads, blocking out the bright morning sun. Horatio continued to lift his leg over and over again, long after every last drop of pee had run out.

"Are you sure you shouldn't check your compass or something?" I said. "It would be really embarrassing to get lost in the woods at a rest area."

"I left the compass in the car."

"Now there's a rookie mistake." I shook my head. "I expected more from you, Camper Anderson."

Horatio stopped to investigate a particularly intriguing scent. John pulled me in for a kiss.

We eventually came out by the designated parking area for large vehicles. Assorted trailers, from massive Winnebagos to little popups, strategically lined up facing the highway entrance. I could only imagine this was so nobody had to try to execute a three-point turn with that many wheels.

"Sweet." John pointed to a truck pulling a turquoise and white trailer shaped just like a canned ham. "I love those trailers—check out the silver wings on the back. I'm almost positive this one's a Shasta Airflyte fifteen-footer, probably from the late '50s or early '60s. Wouldn't it be great to track one down and restore it someday? Or to at least rent one long enough to really get the full experience. Now *that* would be a road trip."

I almost told John that my father had a canned ham trailer connection via one of his sweeper pals and might be able to hook him up. But I stopped myself. If I wasn't careful, this camping thing could take on a life of its own. It would spiral out of control, and before I knew it John and I would have both sold our places. We'd end up living in a canned ham trailer at the trailer park where my father's worst former girlfriend of them all, Dolly, lived. Not to mention the father of one of my former students I'd once accidentally slept with. The less said about canned ham trailers, the better.

I reached one arm around John's waist, gave him a gentle yank in the direction of his car. "Come on, let's get out of here."

. . . . .

As soon as we got back to his Acura, John pulled out three perfectly chilled bottles of water from a cooler in the backseat. I watched him pour most of one into Horatio's monogrammed stainless steel dog dish and put the dish down on the pavement next to the car.

"He doesn't have a travel dish?" I said. "That's so sad."

John opened a water bottle for me, handed it over. "He'll have one soon. He gets to keep his official Camp Winnabone dish. It's part of the package. Don't worry, the humans get Camp Winnabone water bottles."

I leaned back against the car. "Whew, that's a relief."

John opened his own water, held it up. "Cheers."

We tapped plastic. "May the road rise up to meet us," I said.

"May this road trip be the first of many," he said. He tilted his head back, took a long drink.

I took a quick sip and reached for the door. "Let's take this one road trip at a time, okay?"

Our eyes met. John opened his mouth to say something, closed it again.

I climbed back into his car.

"My turn to be DJ," I said once we'd gassed up and were on the road again. "Just give me a minute." I pulled up the music app on my phone and started downloading.

I maxed out my phone's tinny speakers and sang along with Rihanna to "Shut Up and Drive" and with Cyndi Lauper to "I Drove All Night."

I reached over and gave John a pat on the knee. "Join me."

"Play something I know the words to and I'd be happy to."

"Right. Cyndi Lauper lyrics are pretty hard to catch on to."

"And by the way, you don't have to hold your phone up like that. This car has a phone dock attached to the speakers. Right there."

"Of course it does." I wiggled my phone down on the little USB prong. I tapped a miniature album cover on my screen. Tracy Chapman's "Fast Car" filled the air. I sang along with gusto, then joined Sheryl Crow for "Everyday is a Winding Road."

"What?" I said. "You're not getting all judgmental about my taste in music, are you? Come on, I sang that one about the worms crawl in, the worms crawl out, in your stomach and out your mouth and barely judged *you.*"

John stared straight ahead. "Of course I'm not judging your taste in music. It's just that, for me, the best road trip songs are the old classics, whether they're classic camp or classic rock."

"Fine," I said. I downloaded Roger Miller's "King of the Road," which my family and I had sung along to on more family excursions than I cared to count. I cranked up John's fancy speakers and John and I both jumped in. Next we joined Ray Charles for a spirited rendition of "Hit the Road, Jack."

"Happy now?" I said.

"Actually, if it's all the same to you, I wouldn't mind listening to sides E and F of the camp CD."

The thing about trying to have a relationship is that it's the stupid little things that get you. Not politics or religion or if one of you gets cancer whether or not you're going to relocate to Colorado so you can smoke pot during chemo or move to Oregon so you can choose suicide if the chemo doesn't work. One of the biggest fights I had with my former husband Kevin was about whether we were going to go out one night or stay in. A year later he was gone and I couldn't even remember who'd won that particular battle.

"Okay," I said. "This is the best offer I've got. You let me choose the music for the next hour, and then we'll sing along to your camp CD until we get there. By then we'll both have laryngitis, so we can declare our cabin a music-free zone. Deal?"

"Deal."

I belted out "Vacation" by the Go-Go's and John joined in midway through the first chorus. We sang "Love Shack" with the B-52's, knocking away on the roof of the car when we came to the knock a little louder part. By the time we got to Jackson Brown's "Running on Empty" we were really cooking. We had a quick intermission while I downloaded some more songs, then went right into "Drive My Car" by The Beatles and "Little Deuce Coupe" by The Beach Boys.

"Hey," John said. "What about—"

"Uh-uh-uh," I said. "I still have thirty-eight minutes left."

We sang along to "Born to Be Wild" with Steppenwolf and "Born to Run" with Bruce Springsteen and "Truckin'" with the Grateful Dead and "On the Road Again" with Willie Nelson.

We took another quick break for a handful of trail mix, then joined Wilson Pickett for "Mustang Sally." I was pushing the time limit but I managed to squeak in Peter, Paul & Mary's "Leaving on a Jet Plane."

I ended my turn with "Take it Easy" by The Eagles. As we sang the part about a girl, my Lord, in a flatbed Ford, John reached over and held my hand.

"That was fun," he said, once the final chorus was over. "Let's both try to remember that there's always a good compromise."

"Time will tell," I said.

John took his hand back and put it on the steering wheel.

CHAPTER

We'd been off the turnpike for a while now. We didn't need a sign to tell us we were officially in the boondocks.

"Beautiful countryside," John said.

"Mmm." I reached over and turned down the music. "If we pass a restroom, would you mind stopping? Unless they only have outhouses around here, in which case maybe I'll try to hang on until we make it to our cabin."

"I'm sure we'll find something. We should probably fill up with gas again anyway, just to be on the safe side."

We'd made it through side E on the camp CD and were working on side F. We were both pretty hoarse by now. Horatio was getting restless, stretching, circling around on the backseat, flopping back down again with a sigh. It felt like we'd been in John's car for so long I couldn't remember ever not being in it.

"We're making great time," John said. "I bet we'll be able to catch the tail end of breakfast at camp with time to spare."

"Really?" I said. "It feels like it should be at least dinnertime tomorrow by now."

We rode past stretches of farmland scattered with bales of hay and long rows of bumper crop vegetables. Farmhouses and barns and even a silo or two in the distance. Smaller houses built closer to the main road. An occasional turnoff or a sign inviting us to attend a potluck dinner or visit an antique store or find Jesus. And then the woods would close in again for long stretches.

John's built-in GPS gave us a heads up that a right turn was coming up in 1.6 miles.

"Hmm," John said. "I wonder if we should stay on this road until we find a gas station. We can always circle back to our turnoff."

I tapped the GPS menu and searched for gas stations. A short list popped up. Some were not that far away, though I had to admit I was just directionally impaired enough not to have a clue in which direction.

"I think we're okay," I said. "Let's take our exit. Maybe we'll find a cute little village where we can get gas, a bathroom, *and* breakfast."

The GPS gave us our final warning. John put on his blinker, made the turn onto a two-lane road. We wound past a faded house with two bright red

Adirondack chairs on its front porch, a rope hammock slung between two shade trees in the side yard, sheets drying on an actual clothesline.

Trees edged in on us from both sides. We bumped along, the road narrowing and gradually transitioning from paved to once paved.

A cluster of buildings appeared up ahead.

"I spy a gas station," I said in my best preschool teacher voice.

"B-I-N-G-O," John sang.

We pulled into a gas station right out of *Mayberry RFD*. Team player that I was, while John ran his credit card through the slot at the single retro pump, I clipped on Horatio's leash and took him for a quick pee before I went hunting for my own bathroom.

John was staring into the gas nozzle when Horatio and I got back to the car.

"What's up?" I said.

"Strange." John shook his head. "It will only let me pump $1.03 worth of gas."

"Did you forget to pay your credit card bill?"

"Of course not."

"Relax," I said. "I'll just run over and tell somebody inside."

I crossed the dirt-packed gravel to the little building, pulled the door. It didn't budge, so I jiggled the handle. Then I gave the door an unsuccessful push. I could see a guy standing behind a counter. I knocked. He looked at me, pointed to a sign facing me on the plate glass window. *Call 555-648-4522.*

"But," I mouthed. I turned and pointed to John's car.

The guy pointed to the sign again.

I walked back over to John. "Apparently you have to call them. The number's on the window."

John pulled his phone out of his pocket, squinted at the sign, dialed the number, explained the problem.

"What did he say?" I asked when he hung up.

"He told me to try another credit card."

"Do you want one of mine? I paid all my bills last month and everything."

"I have *plenty* of credit. And, just for the record, I pay my bills every month."

"Bully for you," I said.

John found another credit card, scanned it, pumped another $1.03 worth of gas before the pump shut off. He clunked the nozzle back on its cradle a little harder than necessary. He called the guy again.

"Try another card?" I said when he hung up.

He nodded. I grabbed my purse from the car and handed him one of my credit cards. He pumped another $1.03 worth of gas.

We started scavenging through our wallets, on the hunt for more plastic, and managed to come up with four more cards between us.

"This is insane," John said as he divided up our receipts. "It's a good thing my car gets decent mileage—at least we won't run out of gas before we get to camp."

"Maybe the station just likes to spread out the risk," I said. "You know, in case one of the thirty-two cards you use is a stolen card."

"Hmm. I never considered using actual cash."

I dug in the bottom of my purse for my wallet, found a ten-dollar bill, flattened it out. I fed it into the cash slot while John inserted the gas nozzle again.

John pumped another $1.03 worth of gas. The machine spit out eight singles. They started fluttering around like leaves falling from a tree. I snatched them up as ninety-seven cents clanked into the coin return.

"Okay, that's it," I said as I stuffed the change into my purse. "I give up."

John shook his head. "Do you want me to call the guy back and ask if they have a restroom?"

"No thanks. I don't even want to think about the hoops they make you jump through to use it."

Horatio climbed over the console to the driver's seat and stuck his head through the open window. John and I each scratched behind one of his ears.

"Good point," John said. "Maybe we should hold off on breakfast till we get to camp, too. If you want eggs around here, they probably make you stand out by the road and cluck like a chicken."

"Try it," I said. "Let's see what happens."

John smiled, leaned in for a quick kiss. "You know, ten years from now we'll have told our $1.03-at-the-gas-station story so many times we'll both know it by heart. And nobody but us will think it's the least bit funny."

I reached up to brush a pine needle from his shoulder. "I think it's one of those had-to-be-there stories."

He grabbed my hand, pressed it to his cheek. "I'm glad we're there."

. . . . .

We followed a series of Camp Winnabone signs along a winding dirt road. We pulled up in front of a rustic lodge fronted by a long screened porch filled with low Adirondack-style rockers. A friendly woman with curly pigtails that reminded me of the ears of an English sheepdog, which may or may not have been intentional, checked us in. John gave her a credit card. I got ready to hand over one of mine in case she could only charge $1.03 at a time, but apparently this particular problem was isolated to the gas station.

John signed the paperwork. The woman gave him two old-fashioned keys, each attached to a wooden key ring shaped like a cabin. Then she handed us each a schedule printed on a glossy brochure shaped like a dog bone.

She smiled down at Horatio. "Aren't you a hand-some boy," she said in one of those silly voices people use to talk to animals. Horatio wagged his tail in agreement.

The check-in woman held out a purple bandanna in John's direction. Her voice dropped a full octave when she switched back to her people voice. "Please make sure Horatio wears this around his neck at all times when he's outside your cabin. Purple is for beginners, so everyone at camp, especially the instructors, will know that this is his first visit."

John crossed his arms over his chest and put on his serious look. "What are the other categories?"

The purple bandanna dangled from her hand. "While we don't accept dogs with aggression issues, Camp Winnabone recognizes that dogs have different personalities, so we give a red banana to dogs who need more personal space, which reminds our other campers to keep a respectful distance."

"Wow," I said. "That would really come in handy at the school where I teach. Especially for the biters. Not sure it would fly with the parents though."

"What else?" John said.

The woman pulled a laminated chart from a drawer full of bandannas. "Green is for our most experienced canine campers, orange is for service-trained dogs, blue is for our intermediates, and yellow is for advanced beginners."

"With all due respect," John said. "Horatio has had substantial experience with other dogs. He attends puppy play care five days a week, and there's never been a single issue. I bet he'd hold his own with the intermediates, but if you could at least bump him up to advanced beginners, I'd appreciate it."

A look passed over the woman's face and was gone just as quickly. I knew that look. I tried to keep it off my own face at about every third parent-teacher conference.

She smiled a smile that was almost believable. "All our first-time visitors wear purple, regardless of outside experience. But you'll have to bring him back again real soon, at which point we'd be delighted to give Horatio a yellow bandanna." She leaned over the counter and looked down at Horatio. "Won't we give you a yellow bandanna then, sweetie, oh what a good boy you are," she said in her high squeaky dog voice.

Horatio barked in agreement. John took the purple bandanna.

"I still don't agree," John said once we'd stepped away from the check-in desk. He squatted down to tie the bright purple bandanna around Horatio's neck. Then he centered the knot under Horatio's chin, which made Horatio look a little bit like a short, four-legged Cub Scout.

"I don't want to hurt your feelings," I said. "But don't ever do that again. Horatio doesn't care what color his bandanna is, and it only makes you look like an idiot."

John stood up. "How would you have phrased that if you *were* trying to hurt my feelings?"

We looked at each other.

"Let's get some breakfast," he said.

Twenty-one

Our cabin was amazing. The walls were completely covered in knotty pine. Identical pine covered the ceiling, and star-shaped holes cut into the tongue and groove planks allowed recessed lights to shine through. The king-size headboard had been built from logs, most but not all of the bark stripped off. A folded quilt stitched together from hundreds of pieces of dog-themed fabric was draped over the footboard. Next to the human bed was a dog bed, smaller and lower to the floor, but otherwise identical right down to the mini-me log headboard and quilt.

Horatio trotted over and started sniffing his bed.

"Holy rustic," I said.

John picked up a remote from one of the bedside tables. When he pushed a button, the lid of a wooden trunk directly across from the bed opened. Slowly, a flat screen TV arose from the trunk like a vision.

"Okay, maybe not," I said. "But you have to admit the modern amenities are certainly discreet."

John pushed another button and the paddle fan over our bed began to turn.

A bouquet of wildflowers in a cut glass vase perched on a tall dresser along with a card welcoming all three of us—Horatio's name first and mine last. Two Camp Winnabone water bottles and a Camp Winnabone dog dish rounded out the dresser-top tableau. The water bottles and dish were purple to match Horatio's bandanna, I noticed, but to John's credit, he didn't say a word.

John scooped up Horatio's new dish, and the three of us trooped in to check out the bathroom. Double sinks made out of old spatter-painted metal wash bins sat on top of a long slate-tiled countertop. The faucets were reproductions of old water pumps. Next to the sink was an oversize slate-walled shower, and a rain showerhead dropped down from the slate-tiled ceiling. A vintage white claw-foot tub was centered on a bay window with a view of a tiny courtyard.

"Wow," I said. "It's like *Little House on the Prairie* meets *Bath Crashers*."

John pointed through the window. "Look. A fountain."

Sure enough, in the center of the small courtyard a bright red fire hydrant fountain poured water from its side into a vessel filled with flame-colored glass balls.

John opened the door that led to the courtyard and stepped back to let Horatio and me walk through first. A high wooden fence draped with strands of tiny lights gave the courtyard complete privacy. A hot tub was tucked into one corner, two rustic chaises into another. A citronella candle and a book of matches sat on a single low table between the chaises.

I leaned into John. "How about we blow off everything else and just stay in the hot tub until we turn into prunes?"

Horatio sprinted over to a casual grouping of ornamental grasses at the far end of the courtyard and started peeing on each one in turn.

"They certainly haven't overlooked a detail." John pointed again. Conveniently attached to the fence directly above the cluster of tall grasses was a dispenser of poop bags.

"Genius," I said. "Maybe you can find a workshop that teaches him to bag it up by himself."

"Thanks for reminding me," John said. "Let's get the car unloaded fast so we don't miss his clicker training class."

"Wouldn't that be tragic. Okay, how about this—you drop Horatio off at his class while I unload the car. First one who jumps in the hot tub wins."

John didn't say anything.

"What? We don't have time enough for a quick dip while he's at clicker training? How long are the classes anyway?"

"The point is, Sarah, to participate in the classes *with* your dog."

. . . . .

"The point is, Sarah, to participate in the classes
with your dog," I said. I was trudging across the pine
needle-covered path from the parking lot to our cabin
carrying John's ridiculously heavy cooler. Wouldn't
you think they'd allow you to drive right up to your
cabin? But noooo, the road ended at the parking lot.

"The point is, Sarah, to participate in the classes
with your dog," I said again. With each repetition I was
getting a little bit more worked up, but I couldn't seem
to stop myself. I mean, why did John even invite me to
come along if he was going to spend the entire time at
canine camp with his *dog*? And wait till I got my hands
on Lorna once we were both back at Bayberry. What
was that thing she'd said about dropping off the mutt
at archery or his sit-upon making class and John and
me heading back to our cabin for forty-two
uninterrupted minutes of hot sex in our private
meditation garden before we had to pick him up again?
The only part she got right was the private meditation
garden. Assuming, of course, that you were into gazing
at fire hydrants while you meditated.

A golf cart piled with fresh towels and linens driving
in my direction pulled over to one side of the path to let
me pass. I wondered briefly if the housekeeping staff
switched over to snowmobiles during the winter
months.

"Thanks," I said.

"Have a great day," the driver said.

"Time will tell," I said. "Oh, and you have a great day, too."

The pine trees surrounding our cabin completely shielded it from the other cabins. What a waste of a romantic setting. I was huffing and puffing by the time I dropped the cooler on the tiny front porch.

My key was still in the door, the miniature cabin on the keychain dangling, but I decided to leave the door open just a crack anyway. My plan was to hang John's backpack over my shoulders and roll both suitcases straight into the cabin. I was already feeling cranky enough without adding a third trip to the car and back. I mean, really, just because I'd offered to bring in our stuff didn't mean John had to take me up on it.

It turned out that suitcases don't roll quite as easily on a thick bed of pine needles as I'd hoped, but eventually I managed to get everything back to our cabin. I unpacked my suitcase, actually hanging up my clothes in the little knotty pine closet since I had time to kill, taking more than my fair share of the wooden hangers just because I could. I ignored John's suitcase, because I certainly wasn't going to unpack it for him. He could unpack his own nuts, too, as far as I was concerned.

I dropped off my toiletries near the sink with the best light and contemplated my next move. John had suggested I meet him at clicker class, but John wasn't in charge of me. I could take a dip in the hot tub without him if I wanted to. I might even take a nap if I felt like it.

I picked up my dog-bone-shaped copy of the schedule from the dresser, just in case they offered any good classes for people. Sure enough, I found a whole column of Human-Centric Activities.

I scanned the list. *Canine Memories: A Scrapbooking Adventure. Canine Cuisine: Cooking from Scratch is Worth Every Single Solitary Hour It Takes. Cutting Edge Photography Techniques: Capturing Your Dog's Best Angle. Canine Communication: What Your Best Friend is Really Trying to Tell You. It's All in Your Hands: Massaging Your Pooch's Tension Away.*

Really? That was it? That was the entire list of human classes? What kind of a canine camp was this?

I took a deep breath. I'd just wander around and check out the rest of the camp and give John some time to miss me. We were mature, independent adults. When we both got back to the cabin, we'd come up with some kind of compromise that worked for both of us.

I locked my purse in the little safe that was hidden behind a knotty pine panel alongside a small square refrigerator. I wondered briefly if I should haul John's cooler in from the screened porch and transfer its contents to the fridge. Decided that I'd already done far more than my fair share of the work.

After turning the lock from the inside, I pulled the door shut behind me. Belatedly, I thought about the key. I reached to check for it in my pockets, realized my yoga pants didn't have any pockets. Oh, well. John was way too organized to ever forget his key. If I didn't run into him on my walk, I'd just sit on the front porch until he and Horatio got back.

I took off in a new direction so I didn't end up back at the parking lot. The path wound softly through the woods. Every so often I passed a cabin identical to ours. Instead of being numbered, the cabins were named after birds, the type spelled out on a little wooden bird-shaped plaque centered over the door to the porch. I thought this was a nice respite from all the dog stuff, though I imagined the real reason they did it this way was so that everybody didn't fight over who got to stay in the Golden Retriever cabin. Our cabin was named Blackbird. Or maybe it was Blue Jay. Bluebird?

An intersection appeared, along with four signs: LODGE, PARKING, TRAINING FIELDS, WATER-FRONT. I didn't even have to think twice before I turned toward the water.

The lake was crystal clear and even had a pretty decent sand-covered beach. Kayaks, canoes, pedal boats, and a couple of hydro cycles were tied up at a long dock at the shore. Further out, some kind of canine diving class was happening on another dock. Dogs splashed one-by-one into the water as a whistle blew. Their humans cheered as if they were watching Olympic trials.

"Do the dog-free people have to wear bandannas around their necks?" a voice beside me said.

I turned. A nice-looking guy about my age, give or take, grinned at me.

"Ha," I said. "Maybe they could give us a big scarlet *D* with a line running through it to pin to our lapels.

Although we'd need lapels for that. And I guess we'd have to share the color red with the dogs that need their space. Which might actually be fitting." I paused for air. "Sorry. It's been kind of a long morning."

"No need to apologize. I get it. I can't believe I let my girlfriend talk me into this place. At least I brought my fishing pole."

"Damn. I knew I forgot something."

He had a nice laugh. He looked like he was in good shape for our age. I took in his freshly cut hair—thin on top and long on the bottom—and his faded jeans with perfectly executed rips over one thigh. He wore a lightweight plaid flannel shirt with the sleeves rolled up over a green T-shirt with a row of darker green pine trees across the chest.

"Nice trees," I said.

"Thanks. It's my lumbersexual look."

I took a step back. "Excuse me?"

"Lumbersexual. It's the next horizon for the metrosexual. You know, all the urban males are trading in their skinny pants and heading for the great outdoors to find themselves. I'm still a rookie, but just wait, in a few days I should be able to open your beer with my jackknife."

"A chainsaw would be more impressive," I said.

He held out his hand. "Dave Cassidy."

I gave him a closer look to make sure I wasn't having a Partridge Family sighting. "Sarah Hurlihy."

"Ah, begosh and begorra, 'tis the luck of the Irish meeting a lovely Colleen like yourself on this fine camp day," he said. He sounded exactly like my father having one of his Irish moments.

I disengaged my hand from his. "Yeah, well. Nice to meet you, Dave, but I have to go catch up with my boyfriend." I wasn't completely sure he was hitting on me, but I gave *boyfriend* some extra emphasis, just in case.

"Well, if he blows you off for four-legged skateboarding, a bunch of us outcasts are meeting up for happy hour at the picnic tables behind the lodge. Canine camp is the new singles bar, you know. Or at least soon-to-be-single bar. When you're looking at spending the rest of your life competing with a dog for attention, seven times out of ten you're gonna eventually move on."

"Did you just make up those odds?"

He opened his eyes wide. "Would I do that?"

"Some of us," I said, "don't think of it as competing with a dog for attention. Take me, for instance. I'm totally into canine camp."

"Right," he said. But I was already walking away.

"Hey, you don't want to take a quick swim while your boyfriend's ignoring you, do you?" he yelled after me. "It's not a bad beach."

"Oh, go jump in the lake," I said. He was out of earshot, but it felt good to say it anyway. It felt even better that I hadn't been the least bit tempted by this good-looking, flirtatious guy. Our relationship might still need a few little things worked out, but John was definitely the man for me.

Twenty-two

I'd worried that I wouldn't be able to find our cabin again, or even recognize it assuming I did find it, but John's red and white cooler sitting on the porch jumped right through the screen at me. I took a moment to memorize the bird-shaped sign over our screen door.

"Blue jay, blue jay, blue jay," I said.

Before I'd headed back in search of our cabin, I'd followed a well-marked trail from the waterfront to the training fields. Two large grass-covered rectangles sat side by side in a clearing, separated by a long paved strip like a miniature plane runway, a row of split-log spectator benches off to one side. I checked out the low ramps and short tunnels and brightly colored hula-hoops arranged on one of the fields to see if I could pick up any new obstacle course ideas for my students.

Dogs had been lined up with their owners waiting for a turn, but John and Horatio hadn't been among them. The other field was empty, so if the clicker training class had taken place there, it was over.

I didn't think John and Horatio would go to lunch without me, but just in case, next I'd swung by the lodge and found the dining hall. No sign of them, but the good news was I was getting to know my way around Camp Winnabone.

Now, *blue jay* firmly deposited in my memory bank, I wiggled the knob on our cabin door on the off chance that it had somehow managed to unlock itself. No such luck. I opened John's cooler, pulled out a still-chilly bottle of water, sat down on one of the two porch rockers to wait it out.

The crazy thing was that I missed John already. Of course he wanted to take some canine classes with Horatio. Spending time doing separate activities was good for both of us. After we had a nice long bonding lunch together, maybe I'd take a kayak for a spin around the lake. When we met up again for dinner, we'd both have new stories to tell. Which is how non-needy, secure individuals kept things fresh in their relationship.

What was the rush? Eventually camp activities would be over for the day. The hot tub would still be waiting for us. We'd open a nice bottle of wine from John's cooler, grab two glasses, toast each other under the stars. Our courtyard was so private we wouldn't even need bathing suits. I'd turn to face him, slide onto his lap—

My phone rang inside our cabin, snapping me out of one of my better fantasies.

"Hold that thought," I said. I listened to the instrumental version of "If You're Happy and You Know It." I'd recently downloaded this ringtone to bring more positivity into my life and because I thought it was kind of a cute idea for a preschool teacher. *Maybe too cute*, I thought as the final notes played.

My phone went to voicemail. I'd updated my voicemail message, too, on the same optimistic day that I'd changed my ringtone. For longer than I cared to remember, my voicemail had said, *Hello, you have reached Sarah Hurlihy. Leave a message if you want to.* Now it said, in my cheeriest voice, *Hi, It's Sarah. Sorry I missed your call. If you leave a message, I'll even call you back.*

I'd come a long way, baby.

Such a bummer that I'd forgotten to take my phone with me when I locked myself out of the cabin. I could have called Lorna to yell at her for giving me false canine camp expectations. I could have called my father to make sure he was dating again. And I could have pulled up the internet and gotten today's Upgrade Your Dad sweepstakes entries out of the way.

· · · · ·

I rocked on the porch while I drank my bottle of water. Then I rocked some more. And some more. I was just beginning to regret finishing the whole water bottle and considering peeing in the woods for a real camp experience when John and Horatio appeared on the trail that led to our cabin.

"Hey, Camper," I said in my sexiest voice, which wasn't half bad. "What brings you to this neck of the woods?"

"Where have you *been*?" John said.

"Looking for you guys." I kept my voice calm, gave my chair a rock or two. I knew this fork in the road. This was where you either got into a great big stupid fight or you didn't.

John narrowed his eyes. "Why didn't you answer your phone?"

I pointed to the cabin, shrugged, went back to rocking.

"And you didn't want to get out of your *rocking chair* to go inside and answer it?"

"What is your *problem*?" I said. "I'm pretty sure chair-rocking is legal in this state."

John opened the screen door, and the two of them joined me on the tiny porch. "My *problem* is that Horatio and I spent our entire lunch period wandering around looking for you."

"Oh, go eat your nuts," I said. "It's not like you didn't pack enough to live through a famine."

John twisted away from me and reached for the doorknob. When it didn't turn, he jiggled it. A little harder than necessary, I thought. He reached into his pocket for the key, opened the door, stormed inside.

I got up fast so I wouldn't get locked out again. John had disappeared, presumably into the bathroom that I seriously needed to use. Horatio was lapping water from his Camp Winnabone bowl.

I gave him a quick pat. "Don't worry, honey. Grownups fight sometimes. But it doesn't mean they don't love each other, and it *never* means they don't love you."

I spied a single key sitting on the trunk that hid the TV. I knew my key was around here somewhere. In fact, it was well within the realm of possibility that this one might even be my key. I scooped it off the trunk, tucked it into the waistband of my yoga pants. I found my phone.

John shook his head as he came out of the bathroom. "If you wanted to take a shower instead of meeting us at clicker training like you said you would, you could have just said so."

I put my hands on my hips. "What the hell are you talking about?"

"The two wet towels you left on the floor?"

"I didn't *leave* two wet towels on the floor," I said. "I haven't even brushed my teeth since we got here."

We looked at each other.

"Are you sure you didn't just forget you used those towels to give Horatio a quick fluff and buff before class?" I said.

"Of course I didn't *forget*. And besides, he has his own towels."

I considered stomping off to the bathroom, but as much as I appreciated a good high drama exit, John and I appeared to be teetering on the edge of a slope I had no intention of sliding down. "Okay, let's both just take a deep breath here."

"I don't have time to take a deep breath. Horatio has fetching in twelve minutes."

"Oooh," slipped out of my mouth. "Good thing you've got your priorities straight."

John squatted down, unzipped his backpack, grabbed a handful of granola bars. He didn't even offer me one.

He walked over to the trunk. "Did you touch my key?"

"I have no immediate plans to touch anything of yours," I said.

He pointed. "I left it right there."

I shrugged. It's not like stealing John's key was a big enough sin to send me all the way to Hell. I'd probably only have to hang around in Limbo for a few hours. Not even long enough for all those poor little Limbo babies to get to me.

"Fine," John said. "I'll stop by the lodge and ask them for another one until yours turns up."

He opened the door and let Horatio walk through first. John had one foot out the door when he turned around to look at me again.

"Camp Winnabone prides itself on being green," he said. "So, if you don't mind hanging up your towels, Sarah, I'd appreciate it. That way you can use them again the next time."

I looked him right in the eyes. "They're not my towels, *John*. And FYI, I'm not sure I'm planning to hang around long enough for there to *be* a next time. For anything."

CHAPTER

Twenty-three

"Someone's been showering in *our* bathroom," I said in my best *Goldilocks and the Three Bears* voice. What a jerk John was. He'd probably given Horatio a quick sponge bath and topped off his doggie styling mousse so he'd make a good impression at clicker training, and then he'd simply forgotten all about it. As far as I was concerned, John could just use the dog towels when it was his turn to shower. They were probably thicker than the human ones anyway.

I picked up the damp towels from the floor with two fingers and resisted the urge to stuff them into John's suitcase. They smelled oddly spicy. Maybe it was Horatio's styling mousse or even some kind of special dryer sheet the camp laundry used. Or perhaps the smell was actually coming from the cute little saucer of pine cone-studded potpourri sitting on the toilet tank cover.

I opened the door to the courtyard and draped the towels over the backs of the wooden chairs so they could dry in the sun. It was a pretty mature move on my part, if I did say so myself.

Then I looked around the cabin for the other key. If I found it, I could put it somewhere only John would have left it. Then he'd have to apologize to me. I'd accept his apology graciously and then we'd have hot make-up sex and live happily ever after through the rest of our canine camp experience.

I looked and I looked, but I couldn't find the key anywhere. Okay, so we'd just have to come up with another way to get to the hot make-up sex. Next, I considered checking my voicemail. But I didn't really feel like finding out how many messages John had left while he was looking for me. Any other messages would probably only be from my family, in which case they could wait.

"Kayaking it is," I said.

I double-checked that I had both my recently commandeered key and my phone, grabbed one of John's granola bars, and closed the locked door behind me. I breathed in the pine-scented air as I strolled back down to the waterfront. By tonight, John and I would have worked things out. If he ever suggested canine camp again, I'd know better. Maybe I could talk Lorna and Gloria into going on a spa vacation with me instead.

We could turn it into a yearly ritual—John and Horatio would go off to canine camp while I went on an adventure with my teacher friends before the school year started. Secure couples didn't have to do everything together. They weren't joined at the hip. They let each other have their space. John and I would miss each other like crazy instead of driving each other crazy.

When I got to the lake, I ended up going with a hydro cycle instead of a kayak, mostly because I'd never tried one before. New experiences were important, on the water and off. I sprayed on some sunscreen thoughtfully provided by the camp. I locked my phone and cabin key in one of the little dockside lockers, put the little stretchy bracelet the locker key was attached to around my wrist. I buckled up a lifejacket. An attendant untied the hydro cycle from the dock for me, held it steady while I climbed aboard, gave a push to get me started.

I'd expected to go flying across the lake, but the bicycle part of the hydro cycle sat on top of two pontoon-like floats, so it turned out to be more like riding an exercise bike that occasionally moved. It was a good workout though, and my thigh muscles were burning in no time.

I caught up to two women also riding hydro cycles, both wearing little yappy dogs in matching dog print-decorated backpacks.

"Decided to skip fetching, huh?" I said.

"We have much better luck on the water," one of them said.

"Maur*ee-een*," the other one said. "Don't listen to her," she said in my direction. "I'm Donna, by the way."

"Sarah. Nice to meet you both. And don't worry, I didn't hear a word."

"I bet every third person is here for the same reason we are," the hydro cycler named Maureen said. "I mean, where else do you meet someone who doesn't think you spend too much time with your dog?" She reached back to make sure she was still wearing her dog.

"I don't know," her friend Donna said. "We did all right when we went to that fly fishing tournament. Remember?"

Maureen laughed. "Gotta love *those* odds. But most of the guys were way uptight about our dogs scaring off the fish. Face it, the only one who really gets it is another dog lover."

"So," I said. "Are you saying canine camp is the new singles bar?"

"Totally," they said at the exact same time.

"Jinx," they both said. When they laughed, it made me miss my sisters, just for a second.

"You've got to watch it, though," Donna said. "Word is out, so some of the guys who come here are real operators. We met this one guy who told us his name was Mick Dolenz."

"Yeah," Maureen said. "Like we wouldn't remember the names of The Monkees. Well, we have to get going. Farrah and Odette both have pawdicure appointments in twenty minutes."

The two tiny dogs yipped deliriously at the mention of their names. Their owners began the slow process of turning their hydro cycles around.

"A bunch of us are meeting up out behind the lodge for yappy hour," Donna said. "You're welcome to join us."

"Thanks," I said. "But I'm here with my boyfriend. I think we'll probably just hang out in the hot tub and have our own yappy hour. I mean, happy hour."

. . . . .

When my burning thighs couldn't take it anymore, I freshened up my sunscreen and traded my hydro cycle in for a kayak. About three minutes after I started paddling, my arms and shoulders began to protest, but I hung in as long as I could. Then I floated for a while, watching some ducks playing by the shoreline. Closer to me, a couple of geese were fishing for a late afternoon snack, their butts sticking straight up in the air as if they were doing handstands in the water.

"Lose your *boyfriend?*" a guy yelled from a hydro cycle moving slowly in my direction.

I ran through a series of semi-witty responses, but ultimately decided not to waste my breath. As Dave Cassidy pedaled like crazy, his hydro cycle inching forward, I turned my kayak around and dug in hard with my paddle, heading for the dock.

By the time I got back to our cabin, John's cooler had disappeared from the porch. I felt a flash of anger,

as if he'd brought the cooler inside to keep me from
finding him.

Don't be ridiculous, I warned myself. I stood for a
moment, looking at the little BLUE JAY sign over the
screen door, hoping I had the right bird. I walked
across the tiny porch and tried to turn the doorknob.
Locked. I pulled the key from the waistband of my yoga
pants, pictured Dave Cassidy somehow standing just
inside the door. I'd turn to run, but too late. Our arms
would be around each other and we'd fall onto the log
bed—

"Not helpful," I said. I knew what was going on here.
It was so much easier to fantasize about some other guy
than it was to get things back on track with the person
you were actually trying to have a relationship with.

I slid the old-fashioned key into the lock. I paused to
banish all my self-destructive impulses, which took a
long moment or two. Then I let positivity fill me until I
practically glowed like a white light. I even hummed a
few lines of "Kumbaya" for extra good vibes.

I turned the doorknob. Horatio was stretched out on
his bed, snoring lightly. John was sitting on one side of
our bed. He was leaning back against the log
headboard, his legs stretched out in front of him,
watching something on the history channel.

"Hey," I said. "How was fetching?"

He didn't look up.

I resisted the urge to give him the finger and stomp
back out again. Reminded myself that I was better than
that. Decided that it was so not fair that I had to be the
better-than-that one while John got to pout and ignore

me. Wished I'd gotten back to the cabin first so I could have already assumed the pout position by the time John returned to the cabin.

"Listen," I said. "How about if we each just agree to accept half the blame for whatever is going wrong here. You know, on the count of three, we both say we're sorry? Sing a couple rounds of "Down By the Bay" and get this road trip back on track?"

"That was a double gold award-winning small-batch chardonnay," John said. "Not some kind of Tuesday night wine."

I looked at the TV screen for a clue. Army tanks were moving across a desert. I still had no idea what the hell John was talking about, but now I was really thirsty.

I crossed in front of the television, reached for my Camp Winnabone water bottle. "What the hell are you talking about?"

"I was saving that wine for tonight. If you had to drink wine in the middle of the day, don't you think it would have been polite to at least check in to see which bottle was okay to open?"

I took my time filling my water bottle in the bathroom. Then I had a long drink, hoping it would help dissipate the steam coming out of my ears.

I exited the bathroom and stood directly in front of the TV screen. "You mean, what's yours is mine, as long as I don't touch the high end stuff?"

"I didn't say that."

"And I didn't touch your stupid bottle of wine. I've been out on the lake. Being healthy. The only thing I'm drinking is water." I squirted some water into my mouth to demonstrate.

John pointed. A corkscrew and the foil from the top of a wine bottle sat on the other side of the bedspread.

"Are you sure you didn't open it and put it on ice for later?" I said. "You know, and then you forgot about it? Where's the ice bucket anyway?"

John clicked off the TV.

We looked at each other, our silence broken only by Horatio's soft snoring.

"You know," John finally said, "If this relationship is going to work, we both need to tell the truth."

"Okay," I said. "The truth is I don't like you very much right now." I opened the little safe, pulled out my purse. "I need a drink. Which, by the way, wouldn't be true if I'd just finished drinking an entire bottle of non-Tuesday wine. I mean, what kind of control freak assigns a day of the week to his wine? Oh, and just in case you're looking for them, your wet towels are drying in the courtyard."

"I learned a lot today," John said. "Do you know that the first rule of fetching is to make sure it's worth going after?"

We looked at each other.

"Fetch you later," I said. "Way later."

Twenty-four

"Do you know that the first rule of fetching is to make sure it's worth going after?" I said as I made a beeline for the picnic table behind the lodge. I said it over and over again, ramping up the arrogance level with each repetition. I leaned on the word *worth*. I switched the emphasis over to *going after*. I locked my jaw while I said it. Then I made my voice more nasally. I attempted a German accent. Switched to Australian. They sounded pretty much the same.

I sang John's stupid comment to the tune of "Taps." *Do you know. That the first. Rule of fetching. Is to make. Sure it's worth. Going after."*

My eyes teared up as I got into it. *All is done. No more fun. Fetch you later.*

I knew the whole thing between John and me was petty and ridiculous. I mean, when Nancy Drew goes to camp in *The Secret of the Old Clock*, she has real issues to work with. She's only staying at the camp so she can figure out who stole the old clock from a nearby house, which will give her the clue she needs so she can help some deserving heirs get their rightful inheritance. And then, just when she least expects it, she's subdued by the burglars and locked up in the vacant house the clock was stolen from. The stakes couldn't be higher for Nancy.

Wait. I had a mystery to solve here, too. I mean, who used those towels? Who took that bottle of wine? Imagine if Nancy's boyfriend Ned had accused her of the same character-assaulting things. Of course, Nancy and Ned wouldn't be sleeping in the same room, let alone the same bed, and I was pretty sure Nancy was too young to drink the wine she hadn't taken. But the point was that Nancy would know something fishy was going on. She'd get to the bottom of things, and fast. And when she did, Ned would be filled with regret for doubting Nancy. He'd spend the rest of his life trying to make it up to her.

I liked it. It had been a long day, and I had to admit I was too tired for sleuthing now. But first thing in the morning, I'd be all over it.

. . . . .

I'd pictured a little knotty pine bar out behind the lodge where I could buy myself a drink. Instead, two jugs of wine—one red, one white—and some two-liter bottles of soda and seltzer sat on one of the picnic tables surrounding a tall stack of short plastic cups.

I poured a cup of white wine and looked around. Yappy hour was a casual affair. Most of the humans in attendance were wearing wilted versions of the clothes they'd had on all day. Even the dogs' multi-colored bandannas had lost their crispness from repeated dips in water bowls and the lake.

I caught sight of Donna and Maureen, meandered over in their direction. They'd changed into long beachy dresses layered with zip-up hoodies to ward off the late summer chill that was coming in as the sun dropped behind the pines. They'd even put on fresh makeup. Farrah and Odette, their claws painted an identical shade of bright yellow to match their bandannas, were stretched out at their feet, daintily gnawing little green bones shaped like toothbrushes.

Maureen and Donna had a picnic table all to themselves. As soon as I sat down with them, Maureen slid a can of Deep Woods Off across the table to me.

"Thanks," I said. I stood up again, stepped away from the picnic table so our wine wouldn't taste like DDT, gave myself a liberal spray.

Donna held up her plastic cup. "Here's to finding that needle in the haystack—a nice, normal, non-crazy, non-married, non-gay, non-twisted, non-addicted, non-criminal, non-broke, non-younger-women-obsessed, non-boring, non-selfish, non-dog-hating guy."

"Not that she's cynical," Maureen said. She held up her cup. "To finally getting it right."

We touched plastic all around. I took a sip of my wine. Decided John might be right about the Tuesday-night-wine thing after all. Although I was pretty sure this wine fell short of even Monday-night status.

Donna sipped her wine, made a face. "It's wet, I'll give it that."

"Where's your boyfriend?" Maureen said.

I shrugged. "Long story."

Donna took another sip. "It always is."

"Heads up," Maureen said. "Mick Dolenz behind you and headed this way."

"Mind if I join you ladies?" a male voice said behind me.

"Knock yourself out," Donna said.

He walked around the table and sat down next to Maureen. He started to reach his hand out to me and then stopped.

"Ha," I said. "Meet my friend Dave Cassidy."

"You mean you're not really Mick Dolenz?" Maureen said.

"I, for one, am stunned," Donna said.

Whoever He Was opened his mouth to speak, changed his mind, took a sip from his plastic cup.

"Where's your girlfriend?" I asked.

He shrugged. "Actually, I came here with a buddy of mine."

"Who?" I said. "Ed Clapton?"

"I'm pretty sure I just met him," Donna said. "He was hanging around with Bill Dylan."

Maureen, Donna and I started to laugh like we were back in high school, that crazy, out-of-control kind of laughter that doesn't happen often enough once you have bills to pay and a lawn to mow and a life to try to figure out. As soon as we'd start to wind down, one of us would snort or gasp and then we'd rev up all over again.

. . . . .

Maureen and Donna and Farrah and Odette had relocated to the throng of campers gathered around the makeshift bar. Mick Dolenz/Dave Cassidy was still sitting across the table from me.

"So, what's your real name?" I asked. "Not that I'll believe you."

"Stuart," he said.

"Little?" I said.

"Is that a joke?" he said. "Or merely an attempt to crush my last morsel of manhood?"

I shook my head. "Never mind. Preschool teacher. But why do you do it? You know, use an alias when you hit on women?"

He drained the rest of his wine, held up his plastic cup. "S'more?" he said.

"Is that a camp joke?"

He grinned. "Thank you for acknowledging that. And just so you don't get your hopes up, it's the only one I've got."

"That's okay," I said. "I'll take all the isolated yucks I can get today. But you're not answering my question."

He reached for my plastic cup. "And you're not giving me your drink order."

"Seltzer, please," I said.

My back was stiff from too much sitting, but I didn't have the energy to stand up. I shifted around on the hard picnic table bench, wishing it at least had a back to slump against. Yappy hour was in full swing now—just about everybody must stop by on the way to dinner. I listened to the greetings and introductions and laughter as if I were a million miles away.

A woman's voice with a crisp British accent caught my ear. "I've been under the cosh with the DH in hospital with his dicky ticker for the last week. Have only just come up for air and a dose of heavy doggers."

Why couldn't I talk like that? Not that I'd understand what I was saying, but still.

"I had Jane Fonda's dog on my airplane last year," a man was saying. "It only came up to here on my Barkley—tiny little thing."

"I thought Jane Fonda's dog was bigger," a woman said.

"That's Hollywood for you," the man said.

"Thanks," I said as Stuart Little placed my seltzer in front of me.

I took a long sip. "So. Aliases."

He drank some wine, made a face. Put his plastic cup down, rubbed his palms back and forth on the thighs of his perfectly ripped jeans. "This might come as a surprise to you, but there are a lot of crazy women out there."

"And it's easier to take advantage of them if they don't know your real name?"

"No, no, it's not like that at all."

I rolled my eyes.

"Really. It's more like sometimes you just want to be in the moment, you know? No having to tell your whole tedious backstory, all the ins and outs of everything you screwed up to slide all the way back down to where you are now, over and over again, like your whole life has been a bad game of Chutes and Ladders. No worrying about whether or not there has to be, or should be, or could be a tomorrow. There's only you and this person you just met and the rustle of the pine leaves—"

"Needles," I said.

"Needles." He looked up. "And a sky full of not just stars, but the elusive, mysterious, indefinable possibility that one of those stars is going to shine its light right down on the two of you. And somehow, this time around, you're going to beat the odds."

I tried not to look up, but I couldn't stop myself. A rectangle of starless navy blue sky appeared in the space between the pine trees.

"What a manipulative bunch of bullshit," I said.

He sipped his wine, put his cup down again. "It plays a lot better once the stars are out."

I burst out laughing.

"So, what's your story?" he asked. "Is there really a boyfriend?"

"Or is he just a sham to protect me from nefarious men like you?"

"Whoa, nefarious. It's got a nice ring to it, so I think I'll just skip the part where I look it up in the dictionary and take it as the compliment I'm sure you intended."

The sound of John's laughter caught my ear. He was standing by the bar, a plastic cup of sub-Monday wine in his hand. Maureen and Donna flanked him like bookends, and Horatio was rolling around on the ground with Farrah and Odette.

I watched John's lips move. *Do you know that the first rule of fetching is to make sure it's worth going after?* I imagined him saying.

Maureen and Donna hung on John's every word, nodded, flipped their hair.

"Yeah," I said. "The boyfriend is real. At least he was the last time I checked."

Twenty-five

By the time I'd taken three steps away from our picnic table, my tablemate had offered my seat to a woman accompanied by a Golden Retriever with a green bandanna around its neck.

"Sorry to have to break your heart, Stuart Little," I whispered. "But you'll find someone new. Oh, wait, you already did."

The yappy hour crowd was just starting to drift in the direction of the lodge, so I made my way over to the dining hall as quickly as my tired legs could carry me.

I loaded up a recyclable takeout box with salad greens, added some rolls of turkey and Swiss cheese and some carrot sticks from a deli platter. I hoped there weren't any hungry bears craving turkey and Swiss cheese wandering around out there.

The sun hadn't set yet, but in this neck of the woods it had dropped down low enough in the sky that it wasn't doing a whole heck of a lot to keep the dark away either. When I was hanging up my clothes earlier, I'd noticed two flashlights on the shelf of our knotty pine closet. Now I wished I'd thought to bring one of them with me. A sweatshirt wouldn't have hurt either.

Just as I was wondering if I'd be able to identify the blue jay over our porch door in the twilight, I saw the soft glow of an outdoor light coming from our cabin. Leave it to John to think to turn on the light before he left. There was something both reassuring and aggravating about his attention to detail.

I put my takeout box down on one of the porch chairs. Rummaged in my purse for John's key. Wiggled the key around as I tried to find the keyhole.

Before I could unlock it, the door creaked open into the dark cabin.

My heart skipped a beat, then started to race. I reached for the takeout box again, as if I might be able to use it as a weapon. Or maybe even a bribe.

The back of my neck prickled. Was this how Nancy Drew felt right before she was subdued by the burglars? My heart picked up its pace at the thought.

"Hello," I whispered into the dark cabin.

I looked over my shoulder. The outdoor light John had turned on didn't have much reach. The forest of pine trees blocked out most of the remaining light.

I wondered if I had time to run into the cabin, grab a Camp Winnabone flashlight, and run back out again before whatever was inside could grab me.

"Company!" I yelled. My voice sounded as shaky as I felt. "A whole bunch of us!"

An old *Saturday Night Live* sketch flashed back to me randomly, the theme from *Jaws* playing ominously, a shark knocking on the door and saying "Candygram." I shook my head to clear it away.

Nancy wouldn't just stand here like a target. She'd *do* something. I tried to remember where the interior light switch was. Just inside the door on the wall, I was pretty sure.

I counted to three. I channeled my inner Nancy Drew.

I reached one hand inside the dark cabin as quickly as I could.

I flicked on the light. Yanked my hand back out of the cabin as if I'd been electrocuted.

I turned around and ran across the tiny screen porch. I skidded down the porch steps, ran a few feet, tripped on a tree root, ran some more.

I hugged the first tree I came to and slid around behind it so I could use it as a shield. Our little cabin was completely lit up. The front and screen doors were open, giving whoever was in there an easy out.

I waited, poised to run again if I had to.

Nothing happened. Carefully, I rooted around in my purse with one hand and pulled out my cell. I woke up the screen, dialed John's number. "John Anderson," he said after the third ring.

"Someone's in our cabin," I whispered. "Hur—"

I'm out in the woods right now, John's voicemail continued, *taking a break from civilization as we know*

it, but I'll get back to you just as soon as I reenter the
cellular world.

Great. I finally need a man to save me, and he's not
taking calls.

When John's voicemail beeped, I hung up. I mean,
what was the point of leaving a message if he wasn't
going to get it until after I figured things out by
myself?

Or until it was too late. My heart thumped wildly at
the thought.

Minutes passed. Still nothing happened. My heart
calmed down again. I got a little bit bored.

"Come out, come out, wherever you are," I sang
softly.

When my stomach began to growl, I unwrapped my
arms from the tree trunk and ate my dinner.

The bug spray I'd put on at yappy hour was still
holding its own, but it was the thought of the cabin
filling up with mosquitos that finally did it. I tiptoed
across the porch and stood for while in the doorway. I
walked cautiously into the cabin. I looked under the
bed, checked the closet, peeked into the bathroom.
Turned on the courtyard light and stepped into the
garden tub so I could get a good look at the tiny
outdoor space through the bay window.

I'd left the cabin door open while I searched, but I
locked it now and took a careful look around.

The pillow on my side of the bed was gone. So was
the dog-themed quilt that had been draped over our
footboard.

I sniffed the air. Smelled that same spicy smell.

I thought about calling the lodge and asking them to send security. Or a camp ranger or something. And then I'd tell whoever answered the phone to page John so he could come running, overwhelmed with guilt that he hadn't answered my call for help.

Instead, I crawled into bed, pillow-less, and pulled the covers over my head.

. . . . .

I knew I was dreaming, but it didn't make the sparkler in my hand any less real. I was sitting on the roof of our wood-paneled station wagon with my five brothers and sisters. I dragged my sparkler through the air, over and over again, making tiny stars. If I closed one eye, it looked like I was drawing the stars right on the sky.

Because our father's birthday was on the 4th of July, he'd convinced us that the fireworks the Marshbury firefighters set off every year on a float in the middle of the harbor were part of his birthday party. We'd finish up the cake and ice cream at home, drive to the parking lot while it was still light out to make sure we snagged a good spot.

Below us, our parents sat on the hood of our station wagon, our father leaning back against the windshield, our mother leaning back against our father. Our mom, wearing a twin set over pedal pushers and flats, an outfit just like the ones Laura Petrie wore on *The Dick Van Dyke Show*, had her ankles crossed like a movie star.

I leaned back and tried to cross my own ankles just like my mother. Even though it was almost dark, I could still see the dirt around my ankles. Every so often our mother would take out the Lestoil and pour some undiluted onto a raggedy old washcloth. My sisters and brothers and I would take turns standing up on a chair so she could scrub off the dirt that stuck to our feet and ankles like summer socks, along with a layer or two of skin that came with it. For the most part though, our mother left our dirt alone for the summer.

It was a point of honor among my siblings and me to try to avoid all footwear during the summer months. If you burned your feet enough walking barefoot on the hot sand and pavement, after a while you didn't feel a thing, and the soles of your feet took on the consistency of rubber. Whoever had the thickest calluses by the time school started up again was thereby declared the Champion of Summer.

I wanted my mother's flats and her clean, elegant ankles, but I wanted to be this year's Champion of Summer more.

The exact moment the sky grew dark, fireworks began to explode. Every time a new blast went off, my siblings and I would hold on to the luggage rack and lean over the side of the roof.

"Blow, Dad, blow!" we'd yell.

Our father would huff and he'd puff and eventually he'd manage to blow out the lights flashing across the sky like more candles on his birthday cake.

"Heavens to Murgatroyd," he'd say when the last popping light of a firework finally fizzled out. "Now *that* was a tough one." Our father's birthday fireworks magic never got old for us.

Our mother had a quieter kind of magic. She'd poke holes in the lid of a mason jar so we could take turns catching fireflies and releasing them before they got hurt. She'd ask my sisters or me to describe our dream outfit, right down to the polka dot fabric and the faux pearl buttons. We'd never even hear her sewing machine buzzing, but when we woke up on our own birthdays, the exact dress would be waiting in our closet, a big red bow tied around the hanger.

My sparkler was lasting forever. I switched from making stars to circling the sparkler around and around and around. My arm was getting really tired, but if I could only keep going, I could keep our mother safe and sound. I could keep her marooned on our station wagon with us, safely away from sickness and hiding it from us and sharing it with us and hiding it from us again. I could save us all from the gaping hole she would leave in our lives when she died. A hole that would never be filled, no matter how tightly the rest of us held on to one another. No matter how hard or how long we tried to close the gap she'd left.

Another firework went off, this one a massive explosion, powerful enough to send my family and me back through time to the beginning of our father's birthday party again. We gathered around the dining room table like we always did. We sang "Happy Birthday," at the top of our lungs, followed by his favorite "For He's a Jolly Good Father."

When it was my turn, I passed my present, wrapped up in a page of colored newsprint from the Sunday funnies, across the table to him. I'd just started babysitting, and this was the very first present I'd bought with money I'd earned all by myself.

"Make it snappy," my father said. "I can tell this one is gonna be just what the doctor ordered."

I let go of my present. My father held it up to his ear and gave it a shake. "Is it a rosy red convertible with the top down?" he said.

I shook my head.

"Well, that's a fine how-do-you-do." He turned the present upside down and gave it another shake. "Hold your horses, I think I've got it now. Is it that spiffy new bar for the rumpus room I've been trying to talk your mother into?"

I shook my head again.

My father ran his fingers through the hunk of dark brown hair that was always falling into his face. "Well, happy days are here again. Then I guess you got me exactly what I wanted after all, Sarry girl."

I tapped my sparkler in the air as if I were a magician about to pull a rabbit from a hat. My father pulled an old-fashioned key out from behind one of his ears. My newsprint birthday present wrapping had somehow turned into tin. He caught a corner of it and turned the key, over and over again, until he'd peeled off the lid.

My father reached inside, pulled out my present, lined it up on the table with the five other identical bottles from my sisters and brothers that he'd already opened.

Old Spice.

CHAPTER

Twenty-six

I sat up in bed, alone in a cabin in the middle of a camp in the middle of the woods in the middle of nowhere.

I checked the bedside clock. Blinked my eyes a couple times to make sure it really wasn't even 9 P.M. yet.

I turned on the bedside lamp, gave my teeth a quick brush in the bathroom and my sleep-mangled hair a quicker fluff on the way back out, grabbed the single remaining flashlight from the knotty pine closet.

I followed the pine needle-covered path to the parking lot.

There, just like I knew it would be, was the same turquoise-and-white canned ham trailer John and I had seen at the rest area.

My father was sitting on a Kelly green-and-white webbed lawn chair on the ground next to the trailer, the quilt from John's and my footboard wrapped around his shoulders like a stole. John's award-winning small-batch non-Tuesday wine bottle was sitting in our ice bucket on the ground next to him.

A small camp stove lit up the scene. Across from my father, also sitting on green-and-white webbed lawn chairs, were Donna and Maureen. My father and my camp friends were holding marshmallows stuck onto the ends of branches over the little stove.

"One of my sweeper pals," my father was saying, "won a wine rack made entirely out of deer antlers, if you can believe it. He wasn't too keen on it himself, but I bet he could have sold it for a pretty penny out this way."

Farrah and Odette saw me first. They started barking like mini-maniacs.

My father held up his branch in my direction like a salute.

"S'more?" he said.

"What the *hell* are you doing here, Dad?"

He pushed a clump of white hair back from his forehead with his non-marshmallow-roasting hand. "Now that's a fine how-do-you-do. And from one of my very favorite daughters at that."

"Oh, boy," Donna said. "Billy's your *father*? That's weird, on more levels than I plan to think about."

"It's not *that* weird," Maureen said. "Everybody has history."

My father picked up John's wine bottle. "Everybody loves somebody somehow," he sang into the business end.

"Wow," Maureen said. "You sound exactly like Frank Sinatra."

"Bite your tongue," my father said. "That was the Dean. Not that I can't do a fair Frankie Boy when the mood strikes, mind you."

"I don't mean to cut the Rat Pack concert short," I said. "But can I talk to my father alone for a minute?"

Maureen and Donna looked at each other, pushed themselves out of their webbed chairs. My father held out the packet of graham crackers so they could each take one for the road. I broke off two squares of milk chocolate from the Hershey's bar and handed them over.

"Don't forget to enter that sweepstakes every day for me like I showed you," my father yelled as they walked away. "I'll let you sit in my old recliner when you come visit. It's all broken in."

He patted the chair closest to him. "Have a seat, darlin'."

I sat. He wiggled his chair over and handed me one end of John's and my quilt. We listened to the sound of Farrah and Odette's yapping getting softer and softer in the distance. My father pulled out his pocketknife, chose a branch from his stash. He peeled the bark off and carved the end into a point for me. I stabbed a marshmallow, held it over one of the two Sterno candles heating the little camp stove. He speared a new marshmallow for himself.

"So, meanwhile, back in Marshbury," he said. "My Sally had kicked me to the curb for good. And you know I'm not the kind of fellow who takes that sort of thing lying down. I asked her for one more shot at it, so I could pull out all the stops. Reservations at a fancy pants restaurant and not even for the early bird special. We're talking the whole shebang here, soup to nuts."

"Oh, Dad. You didn't." I pictured Sally, her tortured hair, her pointy shoes, her scammy senior sweepers group membership fees, her complete lack of interest in my father.

"It took some convincing, but she finally went along with it. So I put on my swanky duds, polished up my wing tips to within an inch of their lives, even bought her one of those wrist corsages the gals like."

He sighed. "But then, midway through the antipasto, I could feel it in my bones that this dog wasn't gonna hunt."

I held my branch higher so my marshmallow didn't get burnt. "It's okay, Dad. She doesn't deserve you anyway—you're way too good for her. You'll find a new girlfriend in no time. A better girlfriend. One who knows how lucky she is to have you."

"Hold your horses now, Christine, and let me finish my story."

"Sarah."

"Just making sure you're awake, Sarry girl." He leaned back in his chair, pulled his side of the quilt up under his chin. "So there I was, failure to the left of me, failure to the right of me. And then, like a bolt of lightning from the clear blue sky, something came over me. I grabbed that little ring thingamajigger that fits around the napkin, got down on one knee, and asked her to marry me. Even threw in a line or two of Billy Shakespeare's what light through yonder window breaks to impress her. He may not be Irish but he's got a way with words, I'll give him that."

"Oh, Dad, you didn't." I could see it so clearly. Sweepstakes Sally barely looking up from texting while my father got down on one creaky knee and embarrassed himself in front of a restaurant full of people.

I circled my branch like a sparkler to make the image go away. "I'm so sorry."

My father shifted in his webbed chair, sighed another long sigh. "And then, sweet mother of Jesus, butter my Irish butt and call me a potato, she said yes."

. . . . .

"What the hell were you *thinking*, Dad?" I said once we had Carol and Christine on speakerphone and I'd filled them in.

"Nice of you to answer your cell, by the way, Sarah," Carol said. "I've been trying to reach you all day to see if you knew where Dad was."

"He's right here with me," I said.

"No shit, Sherlock," Carol said.

"I cannot believe you guys took off without me again," Christine said. "I love those little canned ham trailers."

"I'm not staying in the trailer," I said. "I'm staying in a cabin with John. Attempting to have a romantic interlude."

"I can't speak for my sweeper pal Ernie," our father said. "But I'll put in a good word for you if you want to get in line to borrow his trailer. She's a real beauty—a 1958 Shasta Airflyte fifteen-footer with silver wings on the back. Between the rear gaucho bed and the convertible vinyl dinette, she sleeps two, four if you don't mind getting cozy."

"I don't *want* to borrow the trailer," I said.

"He means me," Christine says. "God, you're so self-absorbed, Sarah. Thanks, Dad—I appreciate that."

"Kitchenette with an icebox fridge," our father continued. "Bathroom, too, though the place where she's currently anchored doesn't have any hookups. But I'm making do just fine, thank you very much."

"You sure are." I reached for John's wine bottle, lifted it out of our cooler.

"Pour me one, too," my father said. "I think we've got just enough left in there for a couple of wee night caps, if your friends with the dogs didn't drink it all up on us. We've got some pint-sized packets of nuts around here someplace, too."

"You're not screwing things up with John again, are you?" Carol said.

"Of course I'm not," I said.

"You are so amazingly self-destructive." Carol said. "Oh, wait, how did you manage to find Sarah, Dad?"

"Yeah," I said. "How did you find me?"

Our father finished chewing his marshmallow, held out his glass while I poured. "I'm not a Tyrannosaurus Rex, I'll have you know. I simply stopped by the stellular store at the mall last night and had the girl turn my thingamahoosie on. Then I punched your number in. Easy as following a trail of breadcrumbs. I knew you and your fella were heading off for a little alone time, so I thought this would be as good a place as any to hide out and play dead."

Christine yawned. "What do you mean, play dead?"

"Listen up," our dad said. "Here's our plan. We wait till morning breaks, and then one of you kiddos calls Sally up on the telephone and tells her I've gone missing. We let another day or three go by, then you give her another ringaling on the tingaling and tell her it didn't end so well. You fake a quick funeral—nothing fancy, mind you—and then you scatter some fireplace ashes from a boat to the tune of some bagpipe music. And before we know it, she'll forget I ever proposed to her. She's got a lot going on, our Sally."

"I'm going to go out on a limb here," Carol said, "and say that this will never work."

"As long as he's alive," our father said, "a man's word is a man's word. Dead will get me off the hook."

"It's completely insane," I said. "No offence."

Our dad looked up at the sky full of stars. "I'm not asking you kiddos to do it for me. I'm asking you to do it for your mother. She's fine with me dating, but marriage is a whole other ball of wax. And I have no intention of breaking her heart."

. . . . .

The bugle playing "Taps" on the other side of camp sounded sad and distant and eerie, like the end of something bigger than a day. My father and I sat quietly until the final notes drifted away. Then we sat some more while I borrowed his laptop to enter the Upgrade Your Dad Sweepstakes with as many of my new email addresses as I could remember.

I yawned. "How'd you figure out the password to the camp wireless network?"

"Those friends of yours with the little yappers helped me out. Nice girls."

I couldn't think of any more ways to stall, so I handed my father his laptop and my side of the quilt. I pushed my weary body up to a standing position.

"I'll check in with you tomorrow," I said. "I'm sure Carol will have figured things out by then. She always does."

He let out a big beefy yawn. "It's not that I'm opposed to downgrading to a fatal disease. But at my age I don't want to jinx myself either. Especially now that Venus is in retrofit."

I leaned over and kissed the top of his head. "Get some sleep, Dad."

. . . . .

I unlocked the cabin door as quietly as I could. A faint light from the bathroom kept me from tripping over anything. I squatted down to scratch Horatio behind the ears. His back legs twitched a few times, but he didn't open his eyes. "Some watchdog you are," I whispered.

There is nothing worse than climbing into bed with someone you're not getting along with. I slipped out of the clothes I'd been wearing all day and pulled a long, baggy T-shirt over my head. I peeled the covers on my side of the bed back carefully. I slid between the sheets, trying to take up as little space as possible.

I reached for my pillow, remembered I didn't have one, crossed one forearm over the other to create a makeshift headrest.

Beside me, John's breathing was slow and even. I took a quiet breath of my own, then another. Rolled over to one side, then onto my back. Returned to my original position on my stomach. Wondered if I'd have better luck trying to sleep on one of the chaises in the courtyard. The towels had to be dry by now. Maybe they'd be enough to keep me warm, especially if I layered on a sweatshirt or two. But where was the bug spray?

"I suppose you didn't take the quilt from our footboard either," John said.

Twenty-seven

I jumped out of bed like I'd been shot.

I flipped on the overhead lights, swung my half-empty suitcase onto my side of the bed with the strength of Wonder Woman. I yanked my clothes off the hangers in the knotty pine closet, grabbed my stuff from the bathroom counter. Jammed it all into my suitcase along with my laptop.

John sat up and rubbed his eyes. "What are you doing?"

"Don't talk to me." I zipped up my suitcase, found my flashlight again. "Here's your key," I said to clear my conscience. I tossed it onto the trunk. "Mine's around here somewhere."

What a pathetic end to a relationship. At least we had no real ties—we hadn't left so much as an old pair of jeans at each other's places. All we had to do was cut the flimsy cord between us, and go on with our separate lives. I didn't even have a ring to leave on the trunk with the key.

Wait. I hiked up my T-shirt, reached for the little diamond-studded navel ring John had given me after my niece's and my piercing adventure. If I was really honest, sometimes I pretended John's present meant more than it did. But the truth was that it was closer to a diamond earring than a diamond ring.

I was too old for pierced navels, too old for pretend diamond rings, too old for happily ever after fantasies. Clearly I couldn't figure out how to sustain a relationship to save my life. It was time to grow up, face facts, move on.

My eyes met John's. I unscrewed the little ball at the top of the ring, yanked it out quick like a Bandaid, dropped it on the trunk next to the key. It hurt more than I expected, but at least the flash of pain took my mind off everything else that hurt.

John swung his legs out of bed, grabbed his neatly folded pants from the back of a chair, pulled them up over his boxer briefs.

I locked the door from the inside, pulled it shut behind me. I rolled my suitcase across the porch and bumped it down the stairs.

John and Horatio were right behind me. Horatio stretched the length of his leash to pee on a tree trunk.

"Stop," John said.

I walked faster, crossing my flashlight back and forth in front of me to make sure I was still on the path.

"This is ridiculous," John said. "And it's not safe for you to be wandering around alone out here."

I looked over my shoulder. "*Now* you're going to worry about my safety? I've been wandering around by myself since we got here."

"That's not my fault."

I stopped, turned partway around. "Of course it's not your fault. It's never your fault. You do everything perfectly—every hospital corner on your stupid gazillion thread-count sheets, every award-winning small-batch bottle of wine, every individually sized package of trail mix. So why don't you just do me a favor and leave me and my stupid faults alone."

"You have a problem with my *sheets*?"

"You want the truth? I have a problem with all of it. The way you fold everything in your life into such neat little packages. The way you love me enough to drive to Marshbury two-point-three times a week, but not enough to move in with me, even though you know I could never be happy living in the city. You've even convinced yourself that Horatio is the child you never had. I hate to break it to you, John, but he's not a furbaby. He's a *dog*. I work with children all day long, which pretty much makes me an expert on telling kids and dogs apart. And FYI, there's a big difference."

I started walking again, dragging my suitcase behind me.

I heard the occasional crunch of a branch as John and Horatio followed me. "The lodge is closed," John said. "*FYI*."

"So what. I have other options."

"Of course you do. You can pick up your phone, if you haven't already, and wake up your family from a dead sleep. And they'll all jump in the car immediately, no questions asked, to come save you. Which is why, essentially, you're never quite available to form a new, adult family with someone else."

I resisted the urge to cover my ears and sing *lalalalalalala*.

"Oh, go fetch yourself," I said. "*Essentially.*"

. . . . .

The vinyl dinette in the canned ham trailer had converted into a surprisingly comfortable bed, as long as I kept my knees bent and overlooked the fact that I didn't have a pillow. Still, I'd tossed and turned for most of the night. Just as the early morning light was beginning to peek over the pom-pom trimmed café curtains that only partially covered the louvered windows, I'd finally fallen into a deep, dark sleep.

I woke up to the smell of roasting marshmallows.

"S'more?" my father said as I pushed open the trailer door.

"Too early for me. This trailer didn't happen to come with coffee, did it?"

"Of course it did. Ernie set me up with a jar of Nescafe and an entire tin of cream and sugar packets. I think I've got just enough water left in the jug for us to split a cup to get our engines running."

"Great," I said.

"Unless you want to sneak over to camp and grab us a couple cups of the fresh-brewed variety. Not that I'm a coffee snob in any way, shape, or form."

I jumped down to the packed dirt. Even though the canned ham trailer was tucked into one woodsy end of the parking area, now that it was light out I could clearly see John's Acura parked diagonally across from us. He'd made reservations for three more nights. I knew our relationship crashing and burning certainly wasn't enough to throw him off schedule, but in my entire life I'd never wanted to leave a parking lot more. Even on bad dates in high school.

I pulled the hood of my sweatshirt up over my head for camouflage. "Dad? Can we just get out of here?"

He reached for the graham crackers. "We might have to make a run for some more provisions, honey, but other than that I'm feeling cozy right here."

"Well, that makes one of us. Listen, you can hide out at my place as long as you want, but I really need to leave. Fast."

"Ah, young love," my father said. "'Our hearts endure the scourge, the plaited thorns, the way/Crowded with bitter faces, the wounds in palm and side,—'"

"Now, Dad? Please?"

"Just let me finish my morning Yeats. Now where was I? 'We will bend down and loosen our hair over you./That it may drop faint perfume, and be heavy with dew,/Lilies of death-pale hope, roses of passionate dream.'"

I had to admit my father did a mean morning Yeats. But still, my own pale hope stayed dead.

We shared a quick mug of instant coffee. Then I went back inside the trailer, folded the quilt, piled the pillow and flashlight on top of it. My father was just blowing out the Sterno candles in the camp stove when I came out.

"Make a wish," he said.

I scooped up the ice bucket. "I wouldn't know where to start."

My father put the little camp stove inside the trailer. I folded the webbed chairs and tucked them in next to the stove.

"Okay," I said. "I'll walk you part way down the path and point you in the right direction. When you come to the cabin with the blue jay over the screen door, you'll know you've got the right—"

"I've got it down, darlin'." My father wiggled his fingers like Groucho Marx smoking a cigar.

"Oh, right. And don't forget to leave the key you stole."

"Borrowed."

"Just tip-toe onto the porch, put everything down, and get right out of there. I'm sure John and Horatio will be at some stupid sit-upon-making class by now, but still, you can't be too—"

"Nothing wrong with a good sit-upon. Your poor old dad could have used one last night. They don't make the webbing on those chairs like they used to."

. . . . .

Not in a million years did I think I'd ever end up back at the $1.03-at-a-time gas station, but the flatbed truck my father had borrowed from his pal Ernie to pull the canned ham trailer was dangerously close to empty.

"I would have gassed up sooner," my father said, "but I wasn't entirely sure I could steer this baby into position without the trailer knocking a pump or two catawampus. Now that I've grown accustomed to my Mini Cooper, I'm finding this a fair amount of metal to navigate."

I jumped out, directed my father into place with hand signals.

"Stay right there, Dad. I've got this down." I found the change the machine had spit back to me from the ten in the bottom of my purse. This time I fed it exactly $1.03.

Had it only been a day ago that I'd stopped here with John? I was pretty sure our relationship had still been in good shape at that point. So where exactly had we zigged when we should have zagged?

The pump turned off. I fed another dollar into the bill slot, pushed three pennies into the coin slot.

The truth hit me: I was the one who'd ruined our trip. I'd accepted an invitation to canine camp, and then acted like a spoiled brat because it turned out to be all about the dogs.

What was wrong with me that, even when I tried, or at least tried to try, I couldn't figure out how to stay in a relationship and make it work? I mean, John was that needle in a pine forest—a nice, normal guy. So what if he was attached to Horatio. It only proved his capacity for love.

I fed some more money, pumped another shot of gas. John wasn't the problem—I was. Maybe I should get my own dog to practice on.

I'd go to the Marshbury Animal Shelter as soon as I got home, choose the dog with the saddest eyes. A year from now, John and I would run into each other at a dog park somewhere and instantly fall in love again. This time I'd know how to get it right.

Ha—I probably couldn't even handle a hamster. How could I ever risk a dog? At least with my students, if I screwed something up, they had parents to go home to.

Twenty-eight

"Truth be told," our father said, "it sounds a wee bit more complicated than it needs to be. If it's all the same to you kiddos, I still say dead is the only way to fly. It's definitive."

He pushed himself up from my couch and spread his arms wide. "'Eyes, look your last! Arms, take your last embrace! O you/The doors of breath, seal with a righteous kiss/A dateless bargain to an engrossing death.'"

"I know I should know," Christine said, "but who is that?"

"Shakespeare," I said. "Dad's finally forgiven him for being born in England and not Ireland."

"It's not conclusive," our father said. "A clever fellow like that could easily have jumped the pond—it may be that the encyclopedias simply haven't caught up with him yet." He thumped his chest with one palm. "Truth be told, I can feel it right here. Billy Shakespeare has the soul of an Irishman."

"Okay," Carol said. "Back to business. Siobhan's watching the kids, and I don't want to give that boyfriend of hers enough time to sneak over. What's Sally's phone number, Dad?"

Our dad rattled off Sally's number from memory. Christine and I scooted over closer to Carol on my couch. Carol began typing a text.

Sally,

Congrats on saying yes to our father's marriage proposal! All six of his children—who each live nearby, call to check in constantly, and stop by incessantly to keep an eye on his wellbeing!—are deliriously happy that we'll soon be welcoming you into the family! The three of us—Daddy's little girls!—would like to treat you to lunch as soon as possible to celebrate! And also to fill you in on the many and myriad intricacies of our father's finances so that you're in the loop!!

> *Your soon-to-be daughters-in-law!!!*
> *Carol, Sarah, and Christine*

Carol pushed Send.

I shook my head. "That's a lot of exclamation points. Just saying."

"The many and myriad intricacies of his finances?" Christine said. "Why didn't anybody tell me about those?"

"I might have missed them myself," our dad said. "Unless you're counting on some big sweepstakes wins down the road. I'm right there with you on that, by the by. It's just a matter of time till I hit the jackpot—I can feel it in my bones."

"That's arthritis, Dad." Carol put her cell down on my coffee table. "Basically, we want Sally vacillating between being scared off and wondering if Dad's money might just be worth a quick marriage and divorce. If that text reels her in, we've totally got this."

Christine opened the pizza box and distributed paper napkins and plates. I handed out Hawaiian pizza slices all around. Our dad started topping off our wine.

A text from Sweepstakes Sally jingled in before he'd even finished pouring.

Next Tuesday works. Noon at Harbor Heights.

"Wow," I said. "What a charming reply. And how nice of her to pick the most expensive restaurant in town."

"I have to work Tuesday," Christine said.

Carol was already texting a confirmation. "So what. Call in sick, or tell them you have to take a long lunch break."

"I'm free all day," our father said.

"No way, Dad," Carol said. "You're going to sit right here at Sarah's house while we get you out of this marriage. And in the meantime, if Sally calls, do not—I repeat, do not—answer your phone. Sarah, go into your closet and grab the ugliest formal dress you can find."

"Holy moly, you're getting bossy," I said. "Even for you." I popped a chunk of pineapple into my mouth and pushed myself up from the couch. "Fine. I'll be right back. Don't any of you dare touch my pizza while I'm gone."

I had to admit there were more than a few ugly choices hanging in my closet. Why is it that brides always give you that old line about carefully picking their bridesmaids dresses so that you and the rest of the bridesmaids will be able to wear them again? And even worse, why is it that you actually listen to the bride and hang on to the dress, just in case, when the truth was that you weren't all that crazy about wearing it the first time around?

I made my selection, carried the losing dress back out to my little living room.

Christine burst out laughing.

"Funny," Carol said. "So freakin' funny I forgot to laugh."

"You asked for it," I said. I draped my bridesmaid dress from Carol's wedding over the back of the couch and grabbed my pizza.

"What's wrong with it?" Carol said.

"Don't ask me," Christine said. "I distinctly remember being overjoyed at the time that the color was an exact match for my mouthwash."

"And my eye shadow," I said. "Not that I'm proud of that. The shoulder pads were a nice touch, too."

Carol shook her head. "I didn't hear anybody complaining when the shoulder pads made your waists look at least two inches smaller. And besides, like either of your bridesmaids dresses were any better. Okay, fine, we'll use it."

. . . . .

I spent the days freed up by my early canine camp exit quietly walking the beach while I still had time to. I stocked up on single-serving frozen meals, boxes of Annie's Mac & Cheese, cans of yellow fin tuna, preparing for another school year as if it were a blizzard.

Even my father was quiet. He'd pulled the silver truck and the canned ham trailer around to the back of my house to hide them in case Sally drove by. The first night, he'd started out sleeping in my guestroom, but at some point he'd migrated back to the trailer along with the guestroom pillows and blankets.

"Nothing wrong with your guestroom," he said when he showed up in my kitchen the next morning for breakfast. "It's just that the trailer's got more personality."

I knew my guestroom wasn't necessarily a direct reflection on my own lack of personality, but still. "Thanks, Dad," I said. "I needed that right about now."

I caught up on dirty dishes and laundry while my father mowed the small patch of my lawn that wasn't currently covered by a vehicle. I carried my laptop out to the trailer, and my dad and I sat across from each other at the vinyl banquette and entered the Upgrade Your Dad Sweepstakes over and over again.

I walked the beach some more while my father hid out and created some new email aliases. I bought zucchini and yellow squash and broccoli and cauliflower and a couple of tomatoes and an onion and some garlic from the farm stand down the street, swung by the grocery store for a rotisserie chicken and some other stuff. I dusted off my old casserole dish, mixed everything together, and actually managed to come up with dinner.

"Just what the doctor ordered," my father said in between bites. "You've outdone yourself, my dear."

"There may have been an element of luck involved."

He wiped his mouth with a paper napkin. "All my kiddos are good cooks, thank the good Lord."

"Ha. I'm pretty sure the Hurlihy family cooking gene passed me by. I just didn't want my father starving to death while he was staying with me on my conscience. And I should probably think about taking responsibility for feeding myself at some point, too. All that takeout gets pretty old. "

My father closed his eyes as he savored another forkful. "It's been nice spending time with you, honey, even if present circumstances might be a wee bit better for the both of us. It can get a tad lonely rattling around that big old house by myself."

I reached for my seltzer. "I know what you mean. When Kevin still lived here, this place seemed so tiny it was closing in on us, but now there are whole undersized rooms I hardly ever set foot in."

"Good riddance to bad rubbish," my father said. "That husband of yours was not on his best day good enough for you."

"Too bad he's already married," I said. "We could have fixed him up with Sally."

"Now that's a picture I wouldn't buy a ticket to see at the movie theater." My father slid his empty plate away from him on the coffee table, leaned back on my sofa, laced his fingers behind his head. "But that new fellow of yours is a different kind of breed. If you want my best advice, I'd say he's worth trying to hang on to."

"Oh, Dad. I think it's too late. I really screwed things up between John and me this time."

"Nothing a good spit and a polish won't fix."

I shook my head. "He's not exactly a spit and a polish kind of guy. He's more like the turbo steam clean with sulfite-free detergent after extensively researching and finding the best tools available type. And I'm pretty much the can't get her shit together type. Every time I think we've got this thing figured out, I manage to mess it up again. I'm pretty sure it's time to move on with my own life—lots of people live perfectly fulfilling single lives. I just have to let John and me go and accept the fact that I suck at relationships."

"Your mother and I didn't bring up any of you kids to be quitters. And lovely as you are, honey, you're even lovelier when you watch the potty mouth."

CHAPTER

Twenty-nine

At least I had my work. I might be a failure at the
rest of life, but I was a good teacher, maybe even a very
good teacher. And I was ready to dive back in for
another year.

Polly was just getting out of her car when I pulled
my trusty Civic past the clay fish totem pole and the
painted plywood teddy bears and into a parking space.
She waited next to one of the freshly trimmed boxwood
ducks edging the walkway for me to catch up with her.

I looked her up and down. "No broken bones or
anything since we last saw each other?"

"Nope. I think I might be past the accident phase
now."

"Good to hear," I said. "But no pressure. We always
start the year with a fully stocked first aid kit."

"I'm so excited," she said. "Thank you again for taking a chance on me, Sarah."

"Don't thank me again yet. We still need to finish setting up our classroom, which we'll have to do in the mornings, because we have staff meetings and parent meetings in the afternoons. We used to schedule the parent meetings earlier, but now we do them just before school starts, so that the parents don't have time to get out of control and start trying to negotiate classroom switches for any number of random reasons."

"And then next week we'll have actual students?"

I smiled. "Yeah. There is nothing more exciting than the week the kids show up. Not that it ever goes entirely smoothly. At least a couple of the three-year-olds always cry, and double that number for the parents of three-year-olds. So the four- and five-year-olds will start on Monday, and then the youngest kids on Wednesday to give them a shorter week, which makes everybody's transition easier. Beginning with week two, all the kids will go every day, with the third-year students staying for a full day, and the first- and second-year students going home, or to Bayberry childcare, just before lunch."

Polly sighed, like I'd just finished reading her the best story ever. "Oh, I can't wait."

. . . . .

"*What?*" I said when I opened the door to my classroom.

Polly smiled the widest smile I'd seen from her yet.

An entire small fiberglass boat was tucked into the far corner of the room. Nautical-striped pillows cushioned the bottom. The stern was fitted out with a low bookshelf, a smaller bookshelf tucked into the bow.

I walked over to take a closer look. READ READ READ YOUR BOOKS GENTLY THROUGH YOUR LIFE was stenciled in big block letters on one side of the boat. The other side said MERRILY MERRILY MERRILY MERRILY READING IS A DREAM.

"You like?" Polly said.

My eyes teared up. "I *love*. It's incredible. The kids are going to be so excited. And we can sing the original version of "Row, Row, Row Your Boat" with them at circle time and then add the new lyrics. And now that we have a theme, I think we should make a big stuffed octopus from a crazy assortment of striped and polka-dotted knee socks. We can sew shoelaces on each toe so the kids can practice tying their shoes—or maybe even add buckles and strips of Velcro to a couple of them instead, since we'll have so many legs to work with."

I paused for a breath. "Ooh, and one of those little wind-up fishing games would be a great fine-motor activity. And let's not forget about those coffee pod card-holders we made for Go Fish, every preschooler's favorite card game."

Polly was still smiling. "I didn't want to overstep by doing it before I asked, but I was thinking if you liked the idea, I could paint an under-the-sea mural on that wall right over there." She pointed, then reached into her bag. "I made a few sketches."

"Wow," I said. "These are great. I didn't even think to ask you if you could draw when I interviewed you. Why don't you see what we've got for paint in the supply closet and get going on the mural, while I start organizing everything else."

"Aye-aye, boss."

I picked up one of the pillows from the reading boat, spun around with it, put it back down. "We're going to make that show-off new teacher look soooo bad. Wait, we don't have much of a supply budget, so I hope you didn't pay a lot for the boat, and I also hope you got a receipt. Where did you get it anyway?"

"Um, from that show-off new teacher?"

We looked at each other.

"Ethan's a nice guy," Polly said. "I asked him if he had any ideas about where I could find an old boat, and he told me he had one in his storage unit."

"How much?"

"He said we could just have it."

"Right," I said. "Who just happens to have the exact little boat you're looking for in their storage unit and actually gives it to you?"

Polly shrugged. "He even helped me make the shelves with some scraps of lumber he had. He used to be a set designer. And then he made a couple indie films on his own, fell on some hard times, went back to school to reinvent himself, and well, ended up here."

When she blushed, I could tell she knew more than she was telling me. Or maybe it was the thought of Ethan that was making her blush.

"Polly," I said. "Be careful, okay? It's probably just a rumor, but one of the other teachers told me that Ethan and our bitch of a boss are an item."

Polly burst out laughing. "She's his godmother."

. . . . .

Polly stepped back from the bright orange starfish she was painting to get a good look.

"It's perfect," I said. "I'll be right back, okay?"

"Of course."

I knocked on Lorna's former classroom door.

I was so caught up in thinking about what I was going to say to Ethan that it took me completely by surprise when June opened the door.

"Good morning," I said, as if she were a stranger I'd run into on the street, instead of my former assistant that I'd invested an entire school year—not to mention substantial blood, sweat and tears—training. "Is Ethan here?"

When June shook her head, her long silky blond hair rippled around her shoulders. She was so young and beautiful and un-battered by life that she even looked good under fluorescent lights.

"Okay, thanks." I started to walk away. "I'll catch up with him later."

"Sarah?"

I turned around.

"I just wanted to let you know it's okay that you asked for a new assistant. I'm like totally grateful for everything you taught me last year. Ethan's really nice and I think we'll make a good team. And well, I just didn't want to start the school year with any weirdness between us, you know?"

I looked into her big blue cloudless eyes. "You didn't ask to make a switch?"

She shook her head again, setting off another hair ripple. "Of course not. I thought you did. My feelings were a little bit hurt at first, but I'm okay with it now."

"Did Kate Stone tell you I asked for a new assistant?"

"Not exactly. But she kind of implied it, or at least I got the feeling she was implying it."

I thought back to my own conversation with Kate Stone. "That's what happened to me, too. I thought *you* wanted to work with another teacher. You know, if it wasn't for that bitch of a boss of ours, this wouldn't be a half bad place to work. Oh, by the way, be careful—I just found out Kate Stone is your new lead teacher's godmother."

June's eyes were starting to get that spacey look they always got just before she disappeared to meditate. "Yeah, I know. It's cool though—Ethan really appreciates that she gave him a chance when he needed one, but he's also totally down with what a bitch she is. It's like they're family, I guess. You know, nobody loves you more and nobody drives you crazier."

"Ha," I said. "Not that I'd know anything about that."

. . . . .

I found Lorna and Gloria in the kitchen, perusing the coffee pod carousel.

"It's not that they don't all taste pretty much the same," Lorna said, "but I have to admit I'm still overwhelmed by the possibilities. Do I want dark roast or medium roast, and do I trust Paul Newman's coffee legacy to hold up as well as his acting legacy, or do I go with a solid, heartland of America name like Donut House?"

"Actually," Gloria said, "I think Donut House is owned by Green Mountain which is owned by Keurig. And Newman's Own partners with Green Mountain for their coffee, so—"

"Oh, whatever." Lorna closed her eyes, spun the carousel, grabbed a coffee pod.

I took another look at Gloria. "Hey, your hair is back." Sure enough, Gloria's hair had returned from excruciatingly straight to her usual Brillo pad. "See, it didn't last forever after all. Or have you been washing it eight times a day since I last saw you?"

Gloria closed her eyes, reached for a coffee pod. "My youngest wouldn't stop screaming when he saw me, so after substantial research I found out you can revert a keratin treatment without destroying your hair by using a shampoo that contains sodium chloride, aka salt. I broke out the saltshaker and sprinkled a bunch into my favorite shampoo—and voilà. I hated to throw all that hair straightening money down the drain, but in the end I figured it was cheaper than kiddie therapy."

"Well," I said. "It's nice to have your old hair back. You look great."

"Yeah," Lorna said, "as long as you don't look at her feet."

"I hate you," Gloria said. "I am so never telling you anything ever again, Lorna."

I looked down at Gloria's feet. Underneath the flair of her jeans, her feet were completely covered by sneakers and socks.

"Come on," I said. "Just a quick peek."

"Oh, all right." Gloria sat down at one of the round kitchen tables, untied one sneaker, peeled off a long white men's tube sock.

At first I thought she was wearing another sock—a bright blue ankle sock. "Whoa, what did you do to yourself?"

She was already putting her sock back on. "Well, my feet were getting really dry and crackly. And then I saw this post on Facebook saying that the best way to get rid of dry skin on your feet is to mix equal parts blue mouthwash and white vinegar and soak your feet in it. Last time I believe anything I read on Facebook."

"How long did you soak them?" I asked.

Gloria looked up from lacing her sneaker. "Long enough to watch the first three seasons of *Breaking Bad* straight through. My husband took the kids to see his parents for the weekend, and I'd always meant to watch that show, so I finally rented it, and I guess I got a little bit caught up. By the time my feet have faded enough that I can wear flip-flops in public again, we'll have a foot of snow."

"If it's any consolation," I said, "my sister Carol's bridesmaid dresses would have matched your feet exactly."

"Now that Gloria's found the secret recipe," Lorna said, "I'm thinking the three of us can be Smurfs for Halloween this year."

Thirty

Lorna, Gloria, and I were sitting at the outdoor picnic table with the most shade, eating our lunch. Our assistants sat cross-legged on the edge of the playground, eating theirs.

I savored a spoonful of the end of summer casserole I'd just microwaved. Sadly, this was the last of it. It was almost enough to make me want to cook twice in one month.

Our assistants' laughter drifted over to us. "You don't think we're making them feel left out by not sitting with them, do you?" Gloria asked.

"Nah," Lorna said. "This is good. It gives them a chance to talk amongst themselves about us. And it gives us time to figure out how we're going to keep that new, classroom-stealing gigolo of a teacher from showing us all up this year. I mean, it's bad enough that he's sleeping with our bitch of a boss."

I swallowed down another quick bite of casserole. "Okay, time out. Ethan isn't sleeping with Kate Stone. She's his godmother."

"The two things are not necessarily mutually exclusive," Lorna said.

"Eww," Gloria said.

"Oh, stop," I said.

"Okay, I admit it's a bit of a stretch," Lorna said. "But he still stole my classroom."

"I don't think so," I said. "I think it's just Kate Stone's way of turning us all against one another so she's in control. She probably gave Ethan your classroom to piss you off, Lorna. Just like she led June and me each to believe that the other one wanted a classroom switch."

"Oh, no," Gloria said. "Kate Stone asked me at the end-of-the-school year picnic if I'd ever tried one of those new hair-straightening treatments."

"See," I said.

"Crap," Lorna said. "And I walked right into her evil web. The truth is I like my new classroom better after all—it's harder for people to sneak up on me back there. Now I suppose you're going to tell us that we have to be obnoxiously mature and just let the whole thing go?"

"Not at all," I said. "I was actually thinking we should try to get our bitch of a boss to fall for the blue foot thing."

"Good job, honey," Gloria said.

"Pure, undiluted genius," Lorna said. "Oh, Sarah, what a relief—you're still one of us. For a minute there, you had me worried."

Ethan came around the side of the building, carrying his lunch and heading in our direction.

"Okay, you two," I said. "Play nice."

. . . . .

Gloria, Lorna and I got to the staff meeting early, quite possibly for the first time in our respective Bayberry Preschool careers. We even sat in the first row of folding chairs in the all-purpose room that served as meeting space, gym, theater, concert hall, indoor playground, large art project room, and occasional teacher hideout area—another first.

Kate Stone was wearing her boysenberry batik tunic over cropped black pants and Birkenstock sandals. Dangly earrings poked through her thin chestnut shoe polish-hued hair. The backs of her heels were a bit flaky, I was happy to note.

Our bitch of a boss began to tape huge sheets of paper to the walls.

"What fresh hell is this?" Lorna whispered in her best Dorothy Parker imitation.

"Shh," Gloria whispered.

I cleared my throat. "Oh, by the way," I stage-whispered the way we'd planned. "Thank you so much, Gloria, for turning me on to that dry foot remedy. I mean, it sounded so crazy to soak your feet in equal parts blue mouthwash and white vinegar, but my feet haven't been this soft since I was a teenager."

Gloria crossed her sock-covered ankles. "As it was explained to me," she stage-whispered, "mixing the two ingredients together creates a little known but scientifically proven chemical reaction that causes the dry areas, and even most of the wrinkles, to practically melt right off."

"Well," Lorna stage-whispered, "all I know is that it really worked for me—my feet are as smooth as a baby's bottom now. I've heard that the trick is to make sure you rent a few seasons of a television show you've been meaning to catch up on, and just binge watch the whole thing while you soak your feet. Basically, the longer the better."

Kate Stone continued to tape blank sheets of white paper to the walls, so it was hard to tell whether or not she'd taken the bait. Gloria, Lorna, and I turned our fake conversation to other subjects as our colleagues drifted in to join us.

Polly sat down on the seat I'd saved for her. I gave her a semi-subtle eye roll. "Get ready," I whispered.

Our bitch of a boss cleared her throat, all business. When she pressed her hands together in front of her chest, the sleeves of her batik tunic hung like bat wings.

"Welcome," she said. "I trust you all had a restful summer, but not so restful that you'll have difficulty giving Bayberry Preschool your full focus and energy from this moment forward."

Nobody groaned, but we wanted to.

"As some of you already know," Kate Stone continued, "my goal for the year is to keep the entire Bayberry staff on its toes. In that spirit, I'd like you all to stand up now. Walking only on your toes, choose a colored marker from the box on the table."

Since we didn't have a choice, we all tiptoed over to the cardboard box and chose a marker.

"Now, find the sheet of paper with an X in the corner that matches the color of the marker you've chosen."

We rearranged ourselves until we were all color-coded. I took my place with the other greens. I was glad I hadn't chosen the same color marker as either Lorna or Gloria, since we had a slight tendency to crack one another up during the endless stream of activities Kate Stone delighted in coming up with to torture her employees.

"Without talking," our bitch of a boss continued, "and remaining on your toes, line yourself up in front of your sheet of paper in order, from the person who's been with Bayberry the longest, to the most recently hired."

The greens were a pretty smart group, so we immediately began holding up fingers for the number of years we'd worked at Bayberry. I won by a landslide. Ethan and Polly made their thumbs and forefingers into zeros and moved to the end of the line, Ethan in front of Polly. I noticed Ethan balanced on one toe, his other foot dangling just above the floor.

Kate Stone clapped her hands once. "Now, single word answer, beginning with the first person in line, write your number one goal for the school year on the paper in front of you."

I uncapped my marker. Thought about writing SURVIVAL. Reined it in and wrote GROWTH in big green letters instead. Moved to the end of the line and drifted off as the other greens took their turns. Wondered if John and Horatio had enjoyed the rest of their stay at Camp Winnabone, if John might miss me a little bit by now, if staying single for the rest of my life would be growth or survival or just one great big cop-out.

"Can we put our heels down now?" somebody asked. "My arches are really starting to cramp."

"All the better to remind you that teaching is hard work," Lorna said.

A few brave people snickered.

Kate Stone checked her watch. "Heels down. Now, as a group, travel counterclockwise to each of the other sheets hanging on the wall and decide which words should be added to your group's list."

We moved around the room in color-matched packs and collected some goals—innovation, fun, calm, perseverance—to add to the ones we'd already come up with.

"Is she always like this?" Ethan whispered.

"Oh, yeah," I whispered back.

He raised both eyebrows.

"By the way, thanks for the boat," I added belatedly. In my defense, I'd wanted to thank him when he joined us for lunch, but I was afraid that if I did, Lorna and Gloria would want boats, too. "Are you sure we don't owe you anything for it? Polly and I have at least three dollars left in our supply budget."

"No worries. I wouldn't want to think I'd cost you and Polly a six-pack of crayons. Just don't try to take that boat out on the water—it's got some serious leaks in it."

"Damn," I whispered. "There goes our plan for the first day of school."

He grinned his sun-bleached smile. Even though he was ridiculously good looking, I had to admit it was a nice smile all the same.

Lorna sat down in her chair, kicked off one shoe, started massaging her foot.

Kate Stone waited until all the groups were finished writing. "Now, find the notebook that you were undoubtedly prepared enough to bring with you and copy down your list of goals. Post them where you'll see them every day. Memorize them. Ruminate on them. Make your classroom a living embodiment of the wisdom of those words."

Polly and Ethan looked at each other. Ethan circled one finger over his ear, then pointed in the direction of his godmother.

Our bitch of a boss pressed her palms together again, recreated her batik bat wings. "And finally, be sure to pick up your parent meet and greet schedules by noon Wednesday, as your first meeting will be scheduled to begin immediately after lunch. And let's all remember that preschool parents need the same firm, clear limits their offspring do. Their children are lucky to be here. Bayberry Preschool has a significant waiting list. Classroom assignments are not open to negotiation."

Thirty-one

If we had to sit around and wait for Sweepstakes
Sally to show up, Harbor Heights was a nice place for
it. Fall was in the air, but it was still warm enough
today to sit out on the umbrella-studded deck. Not only
did the restaurant have a spectacular peek-through
view of Marshbury harbor, but it also sat up on a little
hill, tucked away from the noise of the passing cars,
flanked by sugar maples already beginning to turn a
kaleidoscope of oranges and golds and reds.

Christine slid a fifth chair over to our table so I
could drape the garment bag containing Carol's
hideous bridesmaid dress over it. Our waitress came by
and we ordered iced tea times three.

"Nice of Sally to be punctual," Carol said. "I killed
myself to get here on time. I had to cut a call with a

client short, then I actually had to wake up Siobhan so she could watch her brothers and sister. I'm pretty sure she's sneaking out at night to see that boyfriend of hers once she's sure Dennis and I are asleep."

Christine laughed. "Remember when we used to do that? Pop out the screen in that window in the corner of the basement, so as soon as it got dark, all we just had to do was—"

"Just wait till Sydney is in high school," Carol said. "It's a whole lot less funny when it's your daughter sneaking out."

I detached, the way I'd learned to when people started talking about kids I didn't have, parental situations I'd never have to deal with myself. Which, with my family's penchant for producing children, was pretty much all the time.

Our iced tea arrived. Carol and Christine's conversation wound down.

"So," Carol said. "Have you worked things out with John yet?"

Christine leaned forward. "I was just going to ask you that."

"None of your beeswax," I said. "Just because the two of you been married for centuries doesn't mean I have to let you get your vicarious thrills from *my* life."

"I knew it," Carol said. "Listen, whatever you did this time, call John and tell him you're sorry before he finally comes to his senses and finds someone else."

I took a sip of tea, put the glass down on the table. "What makes you think *I'm* the one who did something wrong? Never mind, don't answer that."

I was debating whether or not to tell my sisters that John thought I spent too much time with my family, on the off chance that they'd be insulted and take my side for a change, when Sweepstakes Sally showed up.

Carol saw her first. "There she is," she squealed in a voice I was pretty sure I'd never heard come out of her mouth before. "Our new mom!"

The comparison made me cringe, but I had to admit it did the trick. Sally froze. For a moment I thought she'd turn and run. Given the height of the heels she was wearing, it was probably a good thing she reconsidered. She stopped to read a text then joined us at the table.

Sally put her phone down beside her knife, then rested her hand on top of the knife as if she thought she might possibly need a weapon.

"Carol!" Carol said with a big fake smile.

"Christine!" Christine said with the same smile.

"Sarah!" I said in my perkiest voice. "M-I-C-K-E-Y. M-O-U—" I began to sing.

Christine cut me off. "Don't mind our sister," she said. "She can't help herself. She's a preschool teacher."

"Which you have to admit comes in pretty darn handy when you want free advice," I said. "Or a babysitter."

"Get over yourself," Carol said. "Now that Sally's almost in the family, she and Daddy can babysit. We won't even have to call you anymore."

"Can I get you something to drink?" our waitress asked.

Sally took in our three iced teas. "A double martini. Straight up. Three olives."

We sat quietly until Sally's drink arrived, then placed our lunch orders.

As our waitress walked away, Christine held up her iced tea. "To the big day."

Carol and I held up our glasses. Sally took a big slug of her martini.

"So," I said, "have you and Daddy set a date yet?"

A text jingled in. Sally started to reach for her phone, but Carol grabbed it first.

Carol put her thumb on top of Sally's phone, turned off the power, put the phone down next to her own knife. "The Hurlihy family doesn't bring our toys to the table. You can have your phone back once you've finished eating everything on your plate."

Sally opened her mouth to say something, but Christine jumped in first. "The three of us will be bridesmaids, of course, and all of Daddy's grandchildren will expect to be in the wedding, too. Let's see, how many are we up to now?" She started counting on her fingers. "There's Sean, Sydney, Siobhan, Ian, Trevor, Maeve, Lainie, Annie—"

"Etcetera, etcetera, etcetera," I said. "But the most important thing, the thing that would mean the world to all of us—"

"Which, by the way, is an absolute non-negotiable . . ." Christine said.

I reached for the garment bag, began a slow reveal with the zipper.

"We want you to wear our mother's favorite dress!" Carol and Christine said at the same time.

"Owe me a Coke," they both said.

"Owe me another double martini," Sally mumbled.

Carol shook her finger at Sally. "Don't cross your eyes—they'll stick."

I giggled. "Daddy always says that."

Christine opened her eyes wide. "You'll say it, too, won't you, Mommy Sally?"

. . . . .

Carol was driving us back to my place in her minivan so we could give our dad the play-by-play.

"Too bad Sally didn't stick around long enough to eat," Christine said. "She could use a little seafood on her bones."

"Her loss is my lunch tomorrow," I said.

"No way," Carol said. "That doggie bag is for Dad. He's probably starving to death staying with you."

"Thanks," I said.

"I thought Sally should have at least left the tip before she ran off," Christine said.

"Like she wouldn't have been an undertipper," Carol said.

"Yeah," I said. "It wasn't our waitress's fault that Dad has unreliable taste in women. Why should she suffer?"

"The only thing bothering me," Christine said, "is that we insulted Mom's taste with Carol's bridesmaid dress."

"Mom would have been proud of us for looking out for Dad," Carol said. "And let's make it clear—that dress is dated, not ugly. There's a big difference."

"I think we should mail it to Sally," I said. "Just so she has a souvenir to remember us by."

Our father was sitting on my couch leaning over his laptop when we trooped in. I grabbed a spot beside him. Carol and Christine squeezed into the other side of the couch.

Half a dozen senior sweepers, framed in individual boxes, looked out at us from our father's laptop screen.

"What did the Buddhist say to the hotdog vendor?" a white-haired man was saying.

The other seniors leaned forward in their boxes, waiting for the punch line.

"Make me one with everything!" the white-haired man said.

Our dad slapped his knee. "That's Ernie—what a card. He's got a good one about three Irish Catholic dogs walking into a bar, too." He reached under my coffee table for a blob of chewed gum and pressed it over the camera hole.

"Tell me you just put that gum under the table, Dad," Carol said, "and we're not seeing yet another shining example of Sarah's housekeeping skills." She tapped a key a few times to turn off the laptop's microphone.

"Well," our father said as he leaned back between us and got comfortable. "How was your lunch with Sally, girls? I don't need every last detail, but it would be a big help to know whether I'm dead or alive. Ernie doesn't want to rush me, but he's got quite the waiting list for his canned ham. Oh, and you'll be happy to know that my sweeper pals and I just made a unanimous decision to unprescribe from Sally's paid sweepstakes group."

"Good for you, Dad," I said. I handed him the doggie bag.

He opened it and dug right in to Sally's lobster salad sandwich. "Truth be told, free is the right price point when you're on a fixed income. And I'm coming to the conclusion that these big wins can take their own sweet time to materialize. But I don't mind. The biggest prize is having some old coots like myself to keep me company. We're all migrating like a bunch of Canada geese over to some sort of free private group on Fishbook."

"Facebook, Dad," Christine said.

"Fish, face, potato, potahto. The sweepers have come to the conclusion that our Sally is a bit of an operator. Apparently I'm not the only one she's accepted a marriage proposal from these last few weeks."

"Oh, Dad," I said. "I'm sorry. Just remember that even on her best day she wasn't good enough for you."

He gave my knee a pat. "Honey, the fact of the matter is that true love, the kind your mother and I had, doesn't come around all that often. You're lucky to have your socks knocked off by it once in a lifetime."

A text jingled into his phone.

"That didn't take long," Carol said.

Our dad picked up his phone, cleared his throat, read the text to us as if he were reciting poetry.

Not feeling this marriage thing. Let's catch up soon.
P.S. Your daughters need help.

Thirty-two

Polly and I were eating lunch at one of our low classroom tables. We'd picked up sandwiches at Morning Glories to treat ourselves and also to boost our energy for the first afternoon of parent meetings.

A pile of brightly colored empty coffee pods sat on the table between us. I'd taken them outside earlier and spray-painted them. Now Polly was using a permanent marker to draw little eyes and noses and smiles on one side of each pod.

As soon as Polly completed each face, I filled the pod about three-quarters full of potting soil. Then I lined it up with the other finished pods on one of our rubber snow boot trays, which we wouldn't need for at least a couple months, I hoped.

"This is the cutest idea ever," Polly said.

"It doesn't even come close to your reading boat," I said. "Though I have to admit it's fairly inspired, if I do say so myself."

"So, tell me exactly how this will work." Polly handed me another pod.

I scooped some potting soil into it. "Well, next Tuesday, we'll soak the seeds overnight so they'll sprout more quickly. Then Wednesday, the first day all the kids are here, we'll let each of them choose a pod and sprinkle a quarter teaspoon or so of seeds on the soil. Which might sound simple, but just wait."

Polly nodded, as if she were taking notes in her head.

"We'll write their names on the pods for them—I don't think even the older students will be able to write that small. And every day the kids will take turns watering their pod with an eyedropper, which will be great for their hand-eye coordination. But more than that, it will give them something to take care of, to check up on, which will ease their own separation anxiety during the first few weeks of school."

Polly nodded.

"And then, in ten days or so, they'll have their very own . . . chia pets!"

"Chia pets," Polly said. "I was so dying to have one back when they first came out, but I was too embarrassed to buy it for myself."

"That's one of the perks of teaching at a preschool—you get to pretend the toys you buy are for your class-room. Anyway, you and I can have our own, too. I could give you a whole big lecture about modeling being one of the most effective methods of teaching, but the truth is I just want my own chia pet." I sighed. "If it works out, maybe I can upgrade to a goldfish. Though that might be more responsibility than I'm equipped to handle."

"That's so funny coming from someone who's responsible for a whole class full of preschoolers."

I shrugged. "It's a lot different when they have someone else to go home to."

Polly finished drawing the final face. I added a scoop of potting soil. Then I picked up the boot tray and tucked it safely out of the way on a high shelf in our supply closet.

I looked up at our wall clock. "Damn, do you mind running down to the office and grabbing our schedule? Our first meeting starts in ten minutes."

. . . . .

I scanned our meet and greet schedule. Flipped to the next page to check out our class list, noting the kids who were returning. Took a moment to register the students who'd gone missing. Maybe a move, or even a jump to another preschool that was cheaper, or one that their parents thought would give them a better leg up than Bayberry.

"Well," I said. "The good news is it looks like we've got a pair of twins this year, which means one less parent-teacher conference."

"You make it sound like a hand of poker," Polly said.

"In many ways it is. You know, the luck of the draw and all that."

We looked up at the sound of a knock.

There, standing in my classroom doorway, was my former husband, Kevin.

I closed my eyes, opened them again. Tried to absorb the fact that he was still standing there.

It's not like I hadn't just seen his name on our class list. But in my defense, Bayberry Preschool is located in Marshbury, Massachusetts. And Marshbury is dead center in a coastal area known as the Irish Riviera. And Kevin Sullivan is pretty much the Irish Riviera version of John Smith.

The little boy my former husband was holding squealed, tried to wiggle out of his arms.

A woman stepped up beside my ex, holding a wiggling, squealing little girl in her arms. Amazingly, this was my first actual sighting. But I didn't even have to access my inner Nancy Drew to deduce that this was Nicole, aka Nikki, rumored to be chatty as hell and ten years younger than me.

I gave her a quick once over. *Five years younger, tops,* I thought. Either that or I was aging way better than she was.

"Hi!" she said. "I'm Nikki." She looked at Polly. "And this is my husband Kevin."

"And this is Kevin Junior," my wasband said.

"And Nicole Junior!" the woman he left me for said.

I took a moment to ponder the level of narcissism required to have twins and name one after each of you.

Determined that I was being judgmental. Decided I didn't care.

Only in a town the size of Marshbury—small enough that your past never really goes away but hangs around to haunt you for the rest of your natural life—could something like this happen.

"Welcome," Polly said. "It's so great to meet you all." She shot me a quick look, perhaps thinking her lead teacher might want to consider opening her own mouth.

"Sit," I said.

They sat. Polly and I took our seats across from them.

Kevin Junior and Nicole Junior wiggled off their parents' laps, made a beeline for the reading boat. Polly stood up again and followed them, as if this were just an ordinary meet and greet—assistant teacher keeps an eye on children so lead teacher can chat with parents.

"So," Nikki said. "I hope you don't mind that we wrote a long letter to request you as Kevin and Nicole's teacher. Well, actually I wrote it, but big Kevin was behind it one hundred percent. He said the two of you may have had your differences, but he couldn't imagine a better teacher in the whole world."

It was all coming back now. When God was passing out sensitivity chips, my former husband had been absent that day. Perhaps fishing. Or out screwing around.

Our eyes met.

"Wow, huh," Kevin said. "Time sure flies, doesn't it?"

I took a moment to consider his comment. A longer moment to do the math. When my nieces Maeve and Sydney were born a month apart, Kevin was barely out the door. It had seemed beyond unfair that while my sisters were having babies, I was figuring out how to file for divorce.

Maeve and Sydney had both missed the Bayberry age cutoff this year.

The whole time we'd been married, Kevin was never quite ready to have children. I was almost ready, then ready, then more than ready, then getting closer and closer to being too late. But instead of children, Kevin decided to have Nikki.

I found out, he left. And now I had to look at the fact that my replacement was already pregnant with my kids, the ones I never got to have, the ones I'd wanted more than I'd ever admitted, even to myself.

If I'd gotten pregnant instead of Nikki, Maeve and Sydney would have another cousin now, one just enough older to teach them the latest bad word.

I shook my head at my ex. "You are such a freakin' poophole."

"Poophole!" Nicole Junior yelled from the reading boat.

"Poophole!" Kevin Junior echoed.

Their parents just looked at me.

"Polly," I said, "why don't you take Kevin Junior and the two Nicoles down to see the playground. I need to talk to *big Kevin* alone for a minute."

"Sorry," my former husband said when we were alone. "I guess I should have given you a heads up, huh?

When Nikki gets an idea in her head, there's no stopping her."

"Where is your *brain*?" I said. "Never mind, I already know the answer to that."

"They're good kids," Kevin said. "If that's any consolation."

"They both look exactly like you."

"Thanks."

"I didn't mean it as a compliment." I closed my eyes, opened them again. "If you and I had had kids, they might have looked exactly like you, too. They might have had your mannerisms. You know, the way you used to pick your teeth when you thought I wasn't looking, grind them in the middle of the night. The way you used to sit on the toilet reading forever, even though we only had one bathroom."

My ex-husband started looking around the room for something more interesting to focus on. I remembered that part, too.

"And then once we were divorced, sometimes I'd look at our theoretical kids and they'd remind me so much of you that I'd be torn right down the middle between how much I loved them and how much I wished I'd had them with somebody else." I gulped down some air. "Because for the rest of our lives, even if we hated each other's guts, even though you were my *was*band, we'd be forever connected through our children."

"Is there a point to all this?"

"Yes, Kevin, there is a point. I didn't have kids with you. So I don't have to get along with you for their sakes. And I certainly, beyond a shadow of a doubt, don't have to let the kids you had with somebody else into my classroom."

Kevin tilted his head, considering. "No chance I can talk you into it? It would mean a lot to Nikki."

He smiled the smile that used to get to me a long, long time ago.

I pointed to the door. "The office will call or email you with your children's new classroom assignment."

Thirty-three

I was standing in the hallway outside my classroom, staring out the window, waiting for Polly to show up again so I could fill her in on whatever she hadn't already pieced together before our next meet and greet started.

It wasn't even September yet, but a burgundy and ginger leaf was falling from a tree anyway. It floated, suspended in the breeze as if it might be able to fight the force of gravity after all, only to flutter down to the ground to join a scattering of other leaves.

Even on long painful days like this one, life was short, and nothing reminded you like those first falling leaves.

I heard the door to Lorna's old classroom open. If this were last year, I could have told her the whole story fast, like neighbors over a white picket fence, and she would have managed to make me laugh about my former husband and his new wife requesting my classroom for their his-and-her offspring.

"Hey," Ethan said.

"Hey." I turned to face him. He was wearing a narrow tie-dyed tie over a fitted button down blue shirt that was an exact match for his eyes.

"How's it going so far?" I asked.

"One down." He took a few steps in my direction, one foot hitting the ground with a heavier sound than the other. "I cannot believe I just had my first meeting as the big kahuna.

I shook my head. "You are such a surfer boy."

"Not anymore." He looked down at his damaged leg.

"What happened?" I asked.

He looked over my shoulder and out the window. "I blew up a marriage to a woman I loved with all my heart. Then I blew up her phone by drunk dialing her for about a year, and managed to take out a couple of half-baked businesses and a fledgling indie film career along the way. By the time I totaled my car, blowing up my leg wasn't even all that big a deal. Although you should hear me set off the metal detectors at airports."

"I'm really sorry," I said.

"Thanks."

"But why teaching? And at a preschool, of all places?"

He shrugged. "Our boss is my godmother. She showed up at my place one day, read me the riot act and basically scared the living shit out of me. Then she told me that if I got my act together, took some classes while I interned at another preschool, then spent a year somewhere else as a teaching assistant, she'd give me a job. I said yes, mostly because I didn't exactly have any other options rolling in at that point. But the crazy thing is that I like it. What we do *matters* to the kids."

"Yeah, I know," I said. "It really does. Which is pretty much what gets me through when I have days like this."

"What happened?" Ethan asked. "Unless it might happen to me, too, in which case you might want to wait until I have a week or two under my belt before you tell me."

I gave him a quick recap of the Kevin & Nicole/Kevin & Nicole show.

"Men," he said when I finished.

I tried to laugh, but it came out like the bark of a seal pup. "It might have been slightly less jolting if I hadn't just blown up my own relationship. At least I think I did."

Ethan leaned back against the wall. "If you're not sure, find out. Maybe it's not too late."

I turned around so I could see out the window, watched another leaf float briefly, circle down to the ground. "I just don't know if I have the energy to go through it all again, you know? Every time we get it together, it lasts for a while, and then we're back to square one. It's like we know what we want, and we know how to get there, but we can't seem to stay there."

Ethan stepped up beside me so he could see out the window, too. "Obviously, I'm not any kind of an expert here. That being said, I think the Rolling Stones had it right with the can't always get what you want thing. But, to continue the riff, if I've learned one thing, it's that you've got to take the time to figure out what you need. And then you actually have to come out and ask for it, instead of expecting the other person to read your mind."

We turned our heads to look at each other.

"Not bad, surfer boy," I said. "Not bad at all."

. . . .

"Yikes," Polly said when I finally finished filling her in on the story behind our first meet and greet. "And I thought *my* ex-husband was an idiot. I knew something was going on as soon as they walked in, but it was like I didn't get the memo, or speak the same language, or—"

"You did great," I said. "And you have to admit starting off with that one sure made the rest of today's meetings feel pretty tame by comparison."

"Good point. What was that thing Robin Williams said—something like the problem is that God gives men both a brain and a penis, but only enough blood to run one at a time."

"Damn," I said. "I could have soooo used that line earlier."

Polly yawned, stretched her arms up over her head. "So we're done for the day?"

"Yeah, why don't you go home and rest up for tomorrow. I'm going to try to catch that bitch of a boss of ours and tell her she needs to move a pair of twins to another classroom."

"Do you want me to come with you for moral support? You know, united we stand and all that?"

"Thanks, but I think I need to do it on my own. I'm not going to take no for an answer. Bottom line, if Kate Stone wants to keep me as a teacher, she's got to make the switch. So if I'm not here in the morning, you'll know what happened. Give me a call sometime—we'll do lunch."

"Don't even joke about that," Polly said.

In my earlier days at Bayberry, classroom assignments were a more complicated process. Parents lobbied for and against certain teachers, and teachers lobbied for and against certain students, much of it fed by the Marshbury grapevine. Decisions were made by the admissions committee, which then triggered a flurry of requests for classroom changes. It was a long, labor-intensive process, and teachers who complained only ended up on the next year's admissions committee.

These days Kate Stone did the initial interviews and then split the kids up by herself. Rumor had it that she put all the new student names in a hat, pulled them out randomly, and called it a day. I had to admit things actually went a lot more smoothly this way. I also had to admit that once she had a system in place that worked, my bitch of a boss hated nothing more than to make an exception.

I stood in front of Kate Stone's closed door, wondering if I should put this off until after I'd had a good night's sleep. Decided I'd only toss and turn all night thinking about it. Plus the longer I waited, the more ammunition she'd have to argue that it was too late to make a switch.

I took a deep breath, gave my hair a quick fluff, cleared my throat.

I knocked.

"Come in," my bitch of a boss said.

I poked my head into her office. Kate Stone looked up from scraping the sand in a miniature Zen garden on her desk with a rake the size of her index finger.

I'd been hoping for some backup, but her Magic 8 Ball had been relegated to a shelf behind her. *Cannot predict now*, I imagined it telling me.

I cleared my throat again. "Do you have a minute?"

She traced a number in the sand with her rake. "I have five. Exactly."

I closed the door behind me, sat down on the other side of her felled redwood tree desk.

"I realize," I began, "that we have a policy in place about not making classroom switches. But my ex-husband Kevin Sullivan's twins ended up in my class. He said his new wife wrote a letter, but I know you don't take requests . . ."

I waited, but she neither confirmed nor denied.

"So, well, it might have been a Murphy's Law kind of thing. But my point is that it's just not okay. I can handle having his kids in the school, barely, but not in my class. In a nutshell, I need you to move them to another class."

Kate Stone picked up a tiny pebble, tried to balance it on top of another tiny pebble.

She looked up. "Anything else?"

"Well, um, moving forward you might want to add a question about this on our student application. You know, *Have you ever been married to anyone who teaches at Bayberry and might not want your children in her class because even though she's completely over you, seeing your children on a daily basis would be a painful reminder of the large chunk of her life she wasted being married to you?*"

Kate Stone actually smiled. "We'll have to work on the wording, but point taken, Sarah."

I looked up at the Magic 8 Ball. *Yes*, it signaled me belatedly.

I stood up, reached my hand across the table to shake on it. "Thank you so much, uh, Kate."

As I was pushing my chair back in, I couldn't resist a quick peek under my boss's desk.

Peering out between the top of her Birkenstocks and the bottom of her cropped pants was a distinct strip of Smurf blue.

CHAPTER

Thirty-four

I wrote the email in the middle of the night, sitting up in bed with my laptop. I'd left my bedroom window open while I still could, and a cool breeze ruffled the curtain. I pulled the covers up a little higher, imagined I could smell a hint of ocean in the air.

Dear John, I began. Then I deleted the *Dear* so he didn't think I was sending him a *Dear John* letter. Wondered briefly if every man in the world named John held his breath whenever he started to read a letter addressed to him, or if the Dear John thing lost its connotation when John was your actual name.

It was daunting how treacherous even the simplest step could be. But I knew I had to take it anyway.

John,

There's a small dog friendly coffee shop exactly halfway between our places. (You'll be happy to know I actually measured this fair and square via Mapquest and didn't just guess.) I've included the link at the bottom of this email. I'm hoping you'll meet me there at 6 tonight. (If that's not convenient, perhaps you could suggest another day and time that would be?)

I'd like to apologize to you in person, and as my students would say, I got some splainin' to do.

Sarah

I waited until I'd read the email again in the clear light of the morning. Then I pushed Send.

. . . . .

Polly spent the morning finishing her under-the-sea mural. I worked on some more classroom materials and checked email on my phone approximately every three minutes.

When John hadn't responded by 10 A.M., I began to make excuses for him. He'd had a long early morning meeting. The internet at work was down. And he'd also forgotten his phone.

By 11 A.M. I decided John just wanted me to suffer. I turned off my phone. Which lasted for exactly ten minutes. I turned it back on and checked email again. Nothing.

"Are you expecting a phone call or something?" Polly asked.

"Nope," I said.

"Then I'd hate to see how you act when you *are* expecting one." She stepped back from the sea horse she was painting to get a better view.

"Looks great," I said. As soon as she went back to painting, I checked my email again.

"Woo-hoo," Lorna said from our doorway just before lunch. "I got a pair of twins. That's one less parent-teacher conference for me."

Polly and I started to laugh.

Lorna put her hands on her hips. "What's wrong with them?"

"Nothing," I said. "Okay, their father is my ex. You remember Kevin—the jerk I used to be married to?"

"Ooh," Lorna said. "This could be fun."

"Not worth it," I said.

Lorna sighed. "I liked you better when you were still in revenge mode. Remember right after he left, when he said he wanted to come by for the rest of his clothes? And you and your sisters duct-taped the zippers closed on all his pants?"

"Ha," I said. "That was actually my brothers. My sisters did a Lorena Bobbitt reenactment and snipped the ends off all his ties. I just boxed everything up once they were finished and left it in the driveway."

"Wow," Polly said. "That's impressive. When my ex moved out, I only donated his stuff to Goodwill before he could come back for it."

"I hope you took the tax write-off," Lorna said.

Since John was head of an accounting department, the mention of taxes made me check my email again.

"Did you screw things up with your boyfriend again?" Lorna asked.

. . . . .

Polly and I microwaved our single serving lunches and ate them in our classroom.

I held up a tiny paper cup of seltzer. "To a great year," I said, trying not to look at my phone.

"To a great year." Polly held up her seltzer, took a sip. "How do the kids manage to drink out of these little cups?"

I shrugged. "It's good for their fine motor control. Okay, it's really because when they spill one of these, there's a lot less to clean up."

We began our final round of meet and greets. Most of the new parents tried to please us. A few acted like they were interviewing us for au pair jobs. As one set of parents was confirming that their son was toilet trained, he stood up and peed in his pants.

"Byron!" his mother said.

Byron smiled. He stomped a foot in the puddle he'd managed to create on our freshly steam-cleaned area rug.

"Byron!" his father said.

"No worries," I said. "Pee happens. Just make sure you send Byron's change of clothes bag in with him on his first day."

After we finished our last meet and greet, Polly put the final touches on her mural. She washed the brushes and put the paint away in our supply closet.

"Are you sure there isn't anything else I can do?" she asked.

"Just have a great weekend," I said in the most cheerful voice I could muster. "And make sure you rest up for next week."

"Will do." She gathered up her stuff, found her keys.

She stopped at the doorway, turned to face me. "Are you okay, Sarah?"

"Yeah, thanks for asking. I've just got some stuff to work out."

After Polly went home, I alphabetized the books in the reading boat. Decided I was being obsessive. Rearranged the books until they were random again.

I checked my phone one final time. Then I looked up at our classroom clock to verify the time. If I left exactly now, I'd arrive at the halfway point between us just in time to meet John.

Except that he wouldn't be there.

Maybe I should drive to the dog friendly coffee shop anyway. When I got there, I could call him, pretend to be puzzled that he hadn't shown up. No, rather than playing games, I should call him now and ask him directly why he hadn't responded to my email.

Oh, forget it. I'd just go back to my own little house, which oddly enough seemed smaller rather than bigger now that my father had moved back to his own house. I'd find a good movie, microwave a single serving something or other for dinner, pour a glass of wine. After I finished watching the movie, I'd figure out what I was going to do with the rest of my life.

I took one more look around my classroom, shut off the lights, closed the door.

I bent down and picked up an early tri-colored sugar maple leaf from the walkway. I'd take it home with me, iron it between two sheets of waxed paper. When I got back to school on Monday, I'd tape it to one of our windows, the preschool version of a stained glass masterpiece.

I cut across the mostly deserted parking lot.

Leaning back against his Acura, parked directly next to my Civic, was John.

"Hey," I said. "Why didn't you let me drive halfway?"

"I can't do this anymore," he said.

Thirty-five

I froze.

Horatio stuck his head out the open window at the sound of my voice. A puff of wind carried the scent of John's sandalwood soap to my nose like a tease.

John's Heath Bar eyes, a ring of toffee inside a ring of chocolate brown, stared me down.

"I can't do this anymore," he said again. "It's not about who drives the farthest, or how often, or even where it makes the most sense to live."

"It's not?" I fingered the leaf I was holding as if it might hold a clue.

"I've been trying to give you some space, not to push too hard."

"You have?" I said. Not for the first time, I wished life came with directions.

"If you didn't want to go to canine camp, you should have said something. You and I could have taken a road trip somewhere else, and I could have gone with Horatio some other time. Whether or not he's a stand-in child for me, as you so kindly put it, is beyond the point, but I've got to tell you, he's part of the package."

"I get that," I said. "I have no issues with Horatio. At least not anymore. But I have to tell you my family's kind of part of the package, too."

"I have nothing against your family. What I have a problem with is that at the first sign of a problem, instead of hanging around long enough to work things out with me, you throw up your hands and run to them."

I put my hands on my hips. "Well, I have a problem with you having a problem with me opening your stupid award-winning small-batch bottle of chardonnay. Not that I did open it. That was my father, by the way."

"I know," John said. "I ran into him while he was returning everything to the cabin. And you should know that he just called to invite me to dinner on Sunday. Some kind of upgrade your dad thing he wants us to do?"

"Boundaries," I said. "My family seriously needs to work on their boundaries."

Out of the corner of my eye, I saw Kate Stone walking across the parking lot in the direction of her car. "Everything all right, Sarah?" she yelled.

I gave her a thumbs up. "Fine. Thanks for asking."

"Can we finish this conversation at the beach?" I said to John. "You know, stretch our legs, let Horatio run around a little bit?"

"Okay, I'll follow you. But do me a favor and check the rearview mirror occasionally to make sure I'm still with you, okay?"

"Will do," I said. "And if anything weird happens between here and the beach, promise me you'll assume the most positive thing possible, especially as it relates to my character, instead of automatically blaming whatever it is on me, okay?"

. . . . .

A group of women were sitting on beach chairs and laughing, and a couple lugged one small child and one large net bag filled with toys across the sand, but other than that we had the pre-dinnertime beach practically to ourselves.

I kicked off my flats so I could feel the sand between my toes. John considered his shiny work shoes, then took them off and tucked his socks inside. He let Horatio off his leash. Horatio frolicked ahead, then circled back to check up on the rest of his pack.

"He's a great dog," I said.

"Yeah, he is." John put his arm around my shoulders. "What would you think about getting a second dog? It might make things feel more balanced."

"Something to think about," I said.

"Just a thought," John said.

We walked a few steps in silence.

John cleared his throat. "What I really wanted to say is that I haven't wanted to pressure you—"

I slid out from under his arm, stopped walking, turned to face him. "You keep saying that. But what it feels like to me is that you're fractionally committed. You know, a third of the time at your place, a third of the time at mine, a third of the time in our separate corners . . ."

He reached for my non-shoe-carrying hand. "I'm one hundred percent committed. I want to spend the rest of my life with you. I guess I thought you needed some time, that you weren't there yet."

I took a deep breath. "I want to spend the rest of my life with you, too. But where? I have to tell you, there's just no way I could handle living in the city. I'm a total beach town mouse."

John shrugged. "Then I'll move down here. I'll ask my boss if I can work remote—maybe just drive in for meetings. If he doesn't go for it, I'll figure something out."

"Really?"

"Really. And I'm not all that attached to my condo. I'll have to run the numbers, but it might be a good idea to hang on to it, maybe put it into a short-term executive rental program. That way we can use it in between tenants once in a while, you know, like an urban vacation house. But I've got to tell you, I don't think I could live in that little house of yours. Where would we put my pinball machine?"

"Oh, good," I said. "I hate my house."

He laughed. "So, what, we get my condo rented, sell your house, and then look for our own place?"

"Sounds like a plan."

We kissed on it. It started out as a sweet, optimistic kiss, then it turned like the tide, and we were deep in the ocean swimming toward each other.

When we came up for air, Horatio was digging a hole, the sand flying an impressive distance through the air. John and I both reached down to pet him.

I laced my fingers through John's, and the three of us started walking the beach again.

"See, that wasn't so hard, was it?" John said.

I blew out a puff of air. Wondered if I should say it now. Or save it for later. Or forever hold my peace.

John stopped walking. "What?"

"How would you feel about trying to have a baby? You know, us."

"Whoa, I didn't see that coming."

I tried to read his eyes, but I couldn't.

"If I'm really honest," I said, "I've wanted children my whole life. It's who I am. It's probably even in my DNA. And the truth is, I'm almost out of eggs, out of time. I'll be fifty before I know it. Okay, in eight-and-a-half years, but still."

"Wow," John said. "Wow."

"I don't want to pressure you, but it would really help me out if you could say something a bit more specific."

He scratched his head with both hands as if he were trying to make room for a new idea. "Wow, do we want to bring a child into our lives? I guess we'll need to ask and answer that. But at first blush, I'm feeling disproportionately positive."

"John, it's a *baby*, not a freakin' spreadsheet."

He looked out over the ocean. "I guess I thought having kids had passed me by."

"Maybe it has." I crossed my arms over my chest. "At least with me."

He dropped his shoes to the sand, put his hands on my shoulders. "Listen," he said. "It's you that I want, with or without children. So, I don't know, maybe we should just leave it that if it happens, it happens."

"I hate when people say that," I said. "Kids are too important. You either want them or you don't. I need you to know that I want a baby, and that I'd like to try to have one with you. I'm okay if it doesn't work out. But I finally, finally realized that when it's too late, I want to be able to look back and know that I went for it. That *we* went for it, gave it everything we've got. Because I can't imagine anyone in the whole wide world I'd rather have a child with than you."

Our eyes met, held.

"I can't imagine anyone in the world I'd rather have a child with than you either," John said. "Okay, I'm in."

"I love dogs," I said. "If this doesn't work out, we'll have a houseful of dogs. And cats. We can start our own animal shelter if you want. Or we can adopt. I'm open."

We kissed some more, started walking again. Someday I'd tell John about my former husband's twins showing up at Bayberry, but there was no rush. We had a lifetime together to catch up on stories.

We followed Horatio down to the water, and I walked up to my ankles in the semi-warm ocean. John hesitated, then held up one of his pant legs and dipped a toe in.

A wave came out of nowhere, and we jumped out of the way just in time. We moved farther up the beach and walked alongside the high tide line, Horatio stopping occasionally for a particularly good sniff.

The sun dropped lower in the sky. Fall was in the air. I ran my fingers through my hair—not even a hint of frizz.

"So," John said. "What do we do now? You know, in the baby department."

I shrugged. "We throw condoms to the wind. I mean, caution. Actually, both, I guess."

He nodded. "And then we make an appointment with a fertility specialist? I can do some research if you want me to. Or maybe you already know somebody who knows somebody?"

I reached for his hand. "We might want to try it the old-fashioned way first."

I stopped, turned to face him, wiggled my eyebrows. "You know, have sex."

"I like the sound of that."

Thirty-six

John rolled over to check the clock on my bedside table. "Well, I guess we have to get out of bed eventually."

"Yeah, you're probably right." I kicked off my covers and headed for the closed door, naked, to let Horatio in.

"Come here for a minute," John said.

I turned around again, smiled. "No way. I know that look."

Horatio let out a soft whine from the hallway.

"What a good boy," I said as I opened the door. Horatio got a running start with his Greyhound side, used his Yorkie side—short on leg length but long on determination—to make it up on my bed in one leap. He covered John's face with doggie kisses.

I reached for my robe. "How about you take Horatio out, while I rustle us up some early afternoon breakfast?"

"Are you sure?" John said. "Maybe we should step things up gradually here before you do anything extreme like actually cooking for me."

"Oh, go pee with your dog." I picked up his T-shirt from the floor and threw it at him.

Once I'd started a pot of coffee, I opened my fridge to check out the options. Unlike my own personal eggs, the eggs I found in there weren't even close to their expiration date. My refrigerator was all out of bacon though, so I rummaged through the paltry assortment of cans in one of my upper cabinets.

I took a moment to remember where my oven was located. Turned it on to 375 degrees, took out a cookie sheet, covered it with foil, sprayed on some Pam.

I opened a can of Prudence corned beef hash at both ends, serenading myself with the parts of The Beatles' "Dear Prudence" that I remembered. I shoved the whole meat and potato cylinder out one end and onto the cookie sheet. Then I cut it in half with a knife.

With my hands, I shaped the corned beef into two hearts as if it were clay. Then I joined the hearts together at one side. I poked two holes for eyes and made a great big smiley mouth in each heart.

I popped the cookie sheet in the oven. Located a bowl in another cabinet, cracked four eggs into it. Added salt and pepper and some freeze-dried chives. Found a package of shredded cheese in my freezer, hit it on my counter a few times until it loosened up, sprinkled some in.

I poured a cup of coffee and sipped it while I gave the corned beef time to get a head start. Then I scrambled the eggs and everything else together.

I took out the cookie sheet just long enough to fill the holes in John's and my hearts.

. . . .

Claire

Thanks so much for reading *Must Love Dogs: Fetch You Later*, book three of the *Must Love Dogs* series. I hope you enjoyed it, and stay tuned for lots more! Reviews are becoming more and more important in helping readers discover books, so I'd really appreciate it if you'd take the time to share your thoughts in a review or tell a friend. Thank you for your support!

I've included an excerpt of my first nonfiction book, *Never Too Late: Your Roadmap to Reinvention (without getting lost along the way),* in which I share everything I've learned on my journey that might help you in yours. Happy reading!

ACKOWLEDGMENTS

It's been a big transition year for me career-wise, which has made me appreciate my true blue friends and readers more than ever. Thank you, thank you, from the bottom of my heart, for being there and giving me the gift of this amazing writing life. And for anyone reading this right now who might be in the midst of a transition of your own, hang in there and remember that it's all about tenacity—and listening to your heart.

I am beyond grateful to Ken Harvey, Beth Hoffman, and Jack Kramer for reading drafts of this manuscript and making fabulous and much-appreciated suggestions.

Thank you to my Facebook and Twitter friends for your encouragement and willingness to share the details of your own lives. My books are better because of your generosity, as is my life.

Thanks to Mara Jacobs and Colleen Gleason for coaching me so generously on a serendipitous shuttle ride to the airport. Another big thank-you to Pam Kramer for canine and human expertise.

A huge thank you to the wonderful book bloggers and reviewers who so generously shout out my books. I appreciate your support so, so much.

Always and forever, thanks, thanks and more thanks to Jake and Kaden and Garet.

Never Too Late: Your Roadmap to Reinvention
(without getting lost along the way)

Copyright © 2014 by Claire Cook.

JUMPING IN

Reinvention is the theme of my novels. It's the story of my life. Or at least my midlife. Wherever I go and whatever I do—workshops, women's conferences, book events, interviews, visits with friends—it's pretty much what we end up talking about.

I certainly never set out to try to become the mother of reinvention, as a former editor used to call me in a twist on that old band from the '60s, The Mothers of Invention. In fact, it feels more like we're all in this together, muddling along as we try to figure out how to get to that life we really thought we'd be living by now. Perhaps the best thing I have to offer is that I made every mistake in the book and came so incredibly close to never dusting off that buried dream of mine. And now here I am, living the life I almost missed.

Over the course of eleven novels and fourteen years, I've cheered on lots of other women (and a few good men), sharing everything I can think of that might help them in their own reinventions. And I've been lucky enough to hear some incredible reinvention stories, too. Passed them along. Watched them inspire others just when they needed it.

On this particular trip, as I land at the Cancún airport, wade through Mexican customs, climb into a waiting shuttle van, and ride a ferry northeast through turquoise Caribbean ocean to beautiful Isla Mujeres (Island of Women) to give the keynote (on reinvention!) at an annual International Women's Day weekend conference called We Move Forward, it hits me.

Even if I travel and travel and travel, I might never meet you in person. I think it's time to share my journey with you anyway, in hopes that it might help you with your own.

I bump my seriously over-packed suitcase down the ramp and step onto the island of women, ready to soak up the sunshine and stories.

QUICK SUGGESTION

We're all different—our goals and styles and personalities. So if something I say in the pages that follow doesn't resonate for you, ignore it. Turn the page, paper or virtual. Move on.

But if it provokes a strong negative reaction—that Claire Cook has no idea what she's talking about or that's the most ridiculous thing I've ever heard—or if it just really pisses you off, write it down before you move on. Bookmark it. Highlight it. Mark it with a Post-It.

In a week or two, go back and take another look. I don't know about you, but sometimes what I really, really need to hear to get where I'm going is the hardest thing to hear, the thing that initially infuriates me the most.

ROADMAP TO THE STARS

If there were a roadmap to success, we'd all be following it. We'd have it saved on our GPS or made into a poster hanging over our bed. Every book would be a bestseller, every movie would be a mega hit, every blog would have a gazillion followers, every restaurant would have a line snaking out to the street.

There are people who will give you bullet points, action plans, absolute secrets to success. But the truth as I see it is that nobody really knows. What works for you might not work for me. What works tomorrow might not work the next year, or even the next day. If it were easy to be successful, we'd all be doing it.

So you have to create your own roadmap. You have to designate your starting point, figure out your destination, work around the inevitable detours and potholes and traffic jams. You have to stay on the road, even if you don't feel like it. Even if you really need to pee.

It's a huge leap of faith. It's a ton of work.

But it feels awesome when you get there.

REINVENTION DEFINITION

The Merriam-Webster Dictionary presents a range of possibilities when it defines reinvent: "to make major changes or improvements to (something) . . . to present (something) in a different or new way . . . to remake or redo completely . . . to bring into use again."

So make yours a massive, earth-shattering change. Or just the perfect tweak to your existing life. It's your reinvention and you can do it any way you want to.

BURIED DREAM

I've known I was a writer since I was three. I was one of eight kids, and when you grow up in those great big families, you desperately want something that's just yours to make you feel special, to separate you from the pack. I grabbed writer.

My mother entered me in a contest to name the Fizzies whale, and I won in my age group. It's quite possible that mine was the only entry in the three-and-under category, since Cutie Fizz was enough to win my family a six-month supply of Fizzies tablets (root beer was the best flavor) and half a dozen white plastic whale-embellished mugs with turquoise removable handles. (Completely off-topic, but I would give anything to find those mugs again. If you ever see them on eBay or at a yard/garage/tag sale, please let me know!)

When I was six, my first story was published in the Little People's Page in the Sunday paper (about Hot Dog, the family dachshund, even though we had a beagle at the time, the first clue that I'd be a novelist and not a journalist) and at sixteen I had my first front-page feature in the local weekly. I also wrote really bad poetry in high school that I thought was so profound—yep, I was that girl. I majored in film and creative writing in college, studying with some big name writers who gave me lots of positive feedback.

I'd been on this writing road for most of my short life, and it seemed like a straight shot to my destination. I fully expected that the day after graduation, I would go into labor and a brilliant novel would emerge, fully formed, like giving birth.

It didn't happen. Instead, I choked. I panicked. I guess I'd learned how to write, but I didn't know what to write. I felt like an imposter. So, despite all expectations, especially mine, I didn't write much of anything over the next couple decades. Even the prospect of writing a thank-you note would throw me into full-blown anxiety mode. (If I still owe you one from way back then, sorry.)

Hindsight 20/20, I can see that I just hadn't found my stories yet. I write about real women—their quirky lives, their crazy families and friendships and relationships, what they want and what's keeping them from getting it. I simply needed to live more of my own life before I could accumulate enough experience to write my novels. If I could give my younger self some really good advice, it would be not to beat myself up for the next twenty years.

But I did. Most of the time I felt a low-grade kind of angst about not living up to my potential. I did my best to ignore it, but sometimes it would bubble up and I'd feel gut-wrenchingly awful. I tried my hardest to bury the feelings, to forget about my dream.

But it never went away. Writing a novel remained the thing I wanted to do more than anything else in the whole wide world, as well as the thing I was most afraid of.

So I did some other creative things. I wrote shoe ads for an in house advertising department for five weeks right out of college, became continuity director of a local radio station for a year or two, taught aerobics and did some choreography, worked as a bartender, helped a friend with landscape design, wrote a few freelance magazine pieces, took some more detours.

Eventually, I had two children and followed them to their artsy little school as a teacher. I meant to stay for a year or two, but somehow I stayed for sixteen. Sixteen years. I taught everything from multicultural games and dance to open ocean rowing to creative writing. I loved the kids and even won the Massachusetts Governor's Fitness Award for innovative programming. But all along I was hiding from my true passion, the thing I was born to do.

And then one day, propelled by the fierce, unrelenting energy of midlife, the dream burst to the surface again. I was in my forties, sitting with a group of swim moms (and a few good dads) at 5:30 A.M. My daughter was swimming back and forth and back and forth on the other side of a huge glass window during the first of two daily practices that bracketed her school day and my workday as a teacher.

The parental conversation in the wee hours of that morning, as we sat bleary-eyed, cradling our Styrofoam cups of coffee and watching our kids, was all about training and form and speed, who was coming on at the perfect time, who was in danger of peaking before championships, even who just might have a shot at Olympic trial times.

In my mind, I stepped back and listened. Whoa, I thought, we really need to get a life.

And right at that moment it hit me with the force of a poolside tidal wave that I was the one who needed to get a life. A new one, the one I'd meant to have all along. I was not getting any younger, and I was in serious danger of living out my days without ever once going for it. Without even trying to achieve my lifelong dream of writing a novel. Suddenly, not writing a book became more painful than pushing past all that fear and procrastination and actually writing it.

So, for the next six months, through one long cold New England winter and into the spring, I wrote a draft of my first novel, sitting in my minivan outside my daughter's swim practice. It sold to the first publisher who asked to read it. Lots of terrific books by talented authors take a long time to sell, so maybe I got lucky. I've also considered that perhaps if you procrastinate as long as I did, you get to skip some of the awful stages on the path to wherever it is you're going and just cut to the chase.

But another way to look at it is that there were only three things standing in my way all those years: me, myself and I.

My first novel, *Ready to Fall*, was published when I was forty-five. At fifty, I walked the red carpet at the Hollywood premiere of the movie adaptation of my second novel, *Must Love Dogs*, starring Diane Lane and John Cusack. I'm now an actual bestselling author of a whole bunch of novels. Not many days go by that I don't take a deep breath and remind myself that this is the career I almost didn't have.

REINVENTION INTERSECTION

I think we all have that sweet spot—the place where the life we want to live and our ability intersect. For some, the trick is finding it. If you're one of those people, you're still trying to figure out what you want to be when you grow up—at thirty, at fifty, at seventy.

For others, like me, deep down inside you already know what you want, so it's about finding the courage to dig up that dream and dust it off. It's not too late. Dreams don't have an expiration date. Not even a best by date. If it's still your dream, it's still your dream.

. . . . .

Keep reading! Download your copy of the *Never Too Late: Your Roadmap to Reinvention (without getting lost along the way)* or order the paperback. Find out more at ClaireCook.com

Be the first to find out when the next book of the *Must Love Dogs* series comes out. Sign up for Claire's newsletter at ClaireCook.com/newsletter.

ABOUT CLAIRE

I wrote my first novel in my minivan at 45. At 50, I walked the red carpet at the Hollywood premiere of the adaptation of my second novel, *Must Love Dogs*, starring Diane Lane and John Cusack. If you have a buried dream, take it from me, it is NEVER too late!

I've reinvented myself once again by turning *Must Love Dogs* into a series and writing my first nonfiction book, *Never Too Late: Your Roadmap to Reinvention (without getting lost along the way)*, in which I share everything I've learned on my own journey that might help you in yours. I've also become a reinvention speaker, so if you know anyone who's looking for a fun and inspiring speaker, I hope you'll send them to http://ClaireCook.com/speaking/. Thanks!

I was born in Virginia, and lived for many years in Scituate, Massachusetts, a beach town between Boston and Cape Cod. My husband and I have recently moved to the suburbs of Atlanta to be closer to our two adult kids, who actually want us around again!

I have the world's most fabulous readers and I'm forever grateful to all of you for giving me the gift of this career. Midlife Rocks!

xxxxxClaire

HANG OUT WITH ME!

ClaireCook.com

Facebook.com/ClaireCookauthorpage

Twitter.com/ClaireCookwrite

Pinterest.com/ClaireCookwrite

Be the first to find out when my next book comes out and stay in the loop for giveaways and insider excerpts: ClaireCook.com/newsletter.

Made in the USA
Middletown, DE
15 January 2016